Matching Mr. Darcy

Matching Mr. Darcy

A Darcy and Elizabeth Variation

LEENIE BROWN

LEENIE B BOOKS

HALIFAX

Cover design by Leenie B Books. Images sourced from Deposit Photos and Period Images.

Matching Mr. Darcy © 2020 Leenie Brown. All Rights Reserved, except where otherwise noted.

ISBN (print) 978-1-989410-60-8, (large print) 978-1-989410-61-5; (ebook) mobi: 978-1-989410-59-2, epub: 978-1-989410-58-5

Contents

Chapter 15   213

Dedication

To Cindy
who is more of a sister than a friend, and who
tolerates my weirdness and teasing so well. Your
love and support are so greatly appreciated.

Chapter 1

Sitting along the wall with her next youngest sister Mary in a crowded assembly hall, while music played and others danced, was not what Elizabeth Bennet wished to be doing. She would rather be dancing. However, as was always the case at an assembly in Meryton, there were more ladies than gentlemen in attendance, and if she could not dance, then this was the best vantage point from which to watch her two youngest and silliest sisters. The chance of one or the other of them making a fool of themselves was particularly great tonight as there were newcomers to the area whom Lydia would, no doubt, wish to impress and, if things held true to form, Kitty would follow suit.

"Jane seems enamoured with Mr. Bingley," Mary whispered.

"Why should she not be? He is handsome and amiable. I should think it would be quite easy to be fond of a gentleman such as he, especially if he seemed to adore me as he does Jane."

"They do make a lovely pair, do they not?"

"Indeed, they do," Elizabeth agreed.

Tall and thin with an enchanting smile, honey blonde hair, and hazel eyes that were as serene as the morning dew, Elizabeth and Mary's eldest sister, Jane, was the beauty of the county. That she was not married at the advanced age of twenty-three was not due to a lack of offers, but rather a lack of acceptance of any of those offers.

Though Jane, without fail, projected an image of composed calmness, she was not without a longing to be deeply loved and respected by a gentleman who stirred her soul. Not just any gentleman who wrote her poems and worshiped her beauty would do. If Elizabeth guessed correctly, Mr. Bingley was just the gentleman for whom Jane had been waiting.

Earlier tonight, when Jane had danced with Mr. Bingley, her features had been more animated than normal; her smile, wider; her eyes, brighter; and her cheeks had worn a pink hue that would make a prize-winning rose's beauty pale in comparison. Even now, as she danced with Mr. James Lucas, she still carried an air of liveliness that was elevated from her usual pleasant but serene demeanor.

The fact that Jane was smitten with their new neighbour, Mr. Bingley, was evident for one and all to see if they cared to pay attention.

"Mama would be well-pleased to have Jane settled at Netherfield."

"They have only just been introduced," Elizabeth cautioned. Mary was not the sort of sister to get carried away by fanciful, romantic thoughts such as Lydia and Kitty were, but just the same, Mary did on occasion jump to conclusions at a rather rapid pace.

"I only mean if things progress from here. They have had a very good start, despite the company Mr. Bingley keeps." Mary's eyebrows rose over a speaking look.

Mr. Bingley, with his copper curls, cheeks that flamed when exerting himself to dance, and his five thousand pounds a year, had just leased the estate next to the Bennets' estate. He had arrived in the area with his two sisters, the eldest sister's husband, and an excessively handsome and equally as disagreeable friend – a Mr. Fitzwilliam Darcy of Derbyshire.

Elizabeth could not even think the name without a little shudder. Could anyone look more arrogantly aloof than Mr. Darcy, who was, at that very moment, standing along the wall and surveying the gathered throngs of peasants? At least, judging by his look of bored disdain, that is what Elizabeth imagined he was doing.

"Not all the wealth in England would make me wish for such a suitor as Mr. Bingley's friend," Mary added.

"That makes two of us," Elizabeth agreed. "However, we will need to tolerate him for Jane's sake."

She glanced to where Mr. Darcy was arguing about something with his friend and found him looking at her. Quickly, she snapped her attention back to her younger sisters while she listened to see if she could hear what Mr. Darcy was saying to Mr. Bingley.

"...tolerable, but not handsome enough to tempt me; I am in no humour at present to give consequence to young ladies who are slighted by other men. You had better return to your partner and enjoy her smiles, for you are wasting your time with me.[1]"

She gasped as his words slapped her. As if she would agree to dance with the likes of him!

"Lizzy, are you well?"

"Did you hear what he said?" Her heart raced and her anger was threatening to spill out of her eyes as she clutched Mary's arm.

Mary shook her head. "You are hurting my arm."

Elizabeth released her grip on her sister and attempted to smooth away the red marks she had caused. "He – that pompous toad – looked right at me and then said I was tolerable but not handsome enough to tempt him."

"Of all the preposterous things!" Mary declared. "You are second only in beauty to Jane. There is not another in this whole county who

---

1. This quote is taken directly from Pride and Prejudice by Jane Austen

is prettier. The man must be in serious need of spectacles."

Elizabeth could not help but giggle softly at the thought of the haughty Mr. Darcy with round spectacles perched on his nose.

"He would probably glare over them and tsk at us." She lifted her chin and affected a masculine tone. "Not handsome enough. Slighted by other men. Tolerable, I suppose."

"Did he truly say you were slighted by other men?" Mary asked in surprise before casting a glare in the general direction of Mr. Darcy.

"He most certainly did."

"But the only man slighting you is Mr. Darcy!"

"Precisely." She had already danced with several of the gentlemen who were not presently dancing. "Although, to be fair, Mr. Bingley has not yet asked me to dance either."

"But he has danced with several ladies," Mary protested. "Mr. Darcy has not."

That was true. Mr. Bingley had danced nearly every set, save this one, while Mr. Darcy had danced exactly two – one with each of Mr. Bingley's sisters – and he had not even looked happy to do that.

"How do you think Mr. Darcy became friends with Mr. Bingley?" To Elizabeth, they seemed such an odd pair with one being gregarious and the other dour. "Do you imagine it is a family thing like how we are expected to be friends with Mrs. Long's nieces for Mama's sake?"

"I can see no other reason for it unless there is a debt to be paid or a sin to be punished."

Again, Elizabeth found she could not help but giggle at the picture Mary presented of a judge sentencing Mr. Bingley to years of punishment at the hands of Mr. Darcy.

"He must have committed some heinous crime," Mary added with a chuckle of her own.

"Indeed."

"I suppose that, though it is a penalty worse than transportation, being sentenced to be Mr. Darcy's friend is better than death."

"Oh, Mary," Elizabeth said between giggles. "We will cause a scene if you continue." Mary had inherited their father's ability to latch onto a humourous line of thinking and then follow where it led far longer than was entirely acceptable even in private conversation.

"Then, I will not mention how Mr. Bingley is most likely better suited to such a sentence than any other man would be." Mary's eyes sparkled with mirth.

"What do you mean?" Elizabeth asked cautiously.

Mary ducked her head and lowered her voice. "His sisters," she said with a waggle of her eyebrows. "But then, maybe that is it. Perhaps Mr. Bingley is hoping to rid himself of his last unwed sister."

Elizabeth swatted Mary's arm. "That is unkind."

"But possible," Mary protested. "They would suit, would they not? They seem to wear the same expression, and I have seen Mr. Darcy talk to Miss Bingley and, when she tittered about something, he very nearly smiled."

"Truly, Mary, we must stop. I cannot contain my laughter much longer."

Surprisingly, Mary immediately pressed her lips together and sobered. "Mr. Bingley," she hissed with a small tip of her head in reply to Elizabeth's look of surprise.

"Miss Elizabeth, Miss Mary." Sir William Lucas stood before Elizabeth. "This young man would like an introduction. Would that be acceptable to you?"

"Yes, yes, of course," Elizabeth replied.

"Then, may I present Mr. Bingley. Mr. Bingley, this is Miss Elizabeth Bennet and Miss Mary Bennet." Sir William motioned toward them and then with a slight bow, stepped back so that he almost appeared as if he was not going to watch and listen to what followed his introductions.

"I should be greatly pleased if you would both allow me a dance," Mr. Bingley said.

"We would like nothing better," Elizabeth answered.

"Will you honor me with the next set then, Miss Elizabeth?"

"She is an exceptional dancer," Sir William inserted, causing Elizabeth's cheeks, which were already rosy from being nearly caught making sport of Mr. Darcy, to warm further.

"I would be delighted to dance with you."

"Capital! And Miss Mary, can I count on you for the set after that?"

"You may," Mary said simply.

Mr. Bingley extended his hand to Elizabeth. "And then, I shall dance the next after that with your elder sister."

"That will be two sets, Mr. Bingley. Are you certain you wish to make such a statement?" Elizabeth asked.

The gentleman next to her chuckled. "You sound just like my friend. He said nearly the same thing to me not more than ten minutes ago when I told him my plan was to dance with you and Miss Mary and then Miss Bennet."

"Did he indeed?"

"As sure as the floor is beneath our feet, and do you know what I told him?"

Elizabeth shook her head.

"I told him that I would dance a third if there was a third to be had."

Elizabeth's eyes grew wide and excitement danced in her heart. "Do you like Jane so much then? Or were you only saying such a thing to provoke your friend?"

"Can it not be both?" Mr. Bingley's smile was infectious. How was it that Mr. Darcy could remain so somber in the presence of this gentleman who effused joy?

"I will allow that it can be. But is it?"

Mr. Bingley took his place across from her and gave a nod of his head. "Indeed, it is."

~*~*~

"Charles," the eldest of Mr. Bingley's sisters greeted him as he and Elizabeth departed the dance floor. "Caroline would like to dance a second set. Would you be a dear and dance with her?"

"I am sure I cannot. I am engaged for the next set. Could not Hurst do it?"

Mrs. Hurst's eyes shifted from her brother to Elizabeth and back. "She had hoped for you to dance with her."

Mr. Bingley chuckled. "You mean she hoped for Darcy to dance with her, but he will not, and Hurst is likely playing cards."

"Charles," Mrs. Hurst scolded, though it had little effect on her brother.

"Louisa, I would like for you to meet Miss Elizabeth Bennet. Miss Elizabeth, this is my sister Mrs. Hurst. Come. I will introduce you to my sister Caroline as well." He looked to where Mary sat. "Miss Mary, you must join us. Louisa, this is Miss Elizabeth's sister, Miss Mary. Miss Mary, my sister, Mrs. Hurst. Come. Come." He herded them all a distance down the room.

Mr. Bingley seemed the sort of gentleman to get what he wanted and he got it how he wanted it. Perhaps it was that sort of spirit which made it easier for him to tolerate a friend such as Mr. Darcy.

"Caroline, I would like you to meet some new friends and neighbours. This is Miss Elizabeth and Miss Mary Bennet of Longbourn. Miss Mary, Miss Elizabeth, my sister, Miss Bingley."

His sister's lips curled into a polite smile. "It is a pleasure."

"Darcy," Mr. Bingley said, turning to his friend and giving the man a cunning grin, which caused his friend's scowl to deepen. "I would like you to meet Miss Elizabeth and Miss Mary. Ladies, this frightening looking fellow is Mr. Fitzwilliam Darcy of Derbyshire."

"Frightening looking? Really, Charles," Miss Bingley protested. "It is a wonder Mr. Darcy retains you as a friend with such treatment."

Elizabeth bit the inside of her cheek to keep from laughing. The greater wonder was why Mr. Bingley kept a friend like Mr. Darcy rather than the other way around. However, from the way Miss Bingley smiled at Mr. Darcy, it was evident that the lady was hoping to win that gentleman's favour by coming to his aid.

"I am happy to make your acquaintance," Mr. Darcy said with a bow, his eyes meeting Elizabeth's and lingering.

His voice, when he was not being insulting, was the sort that washed easily over a lady and caused her heart to flutter. That, when combined with his handsome features, his imposing figure, and those blue eyes that seemed to look straight through a lady to examine her soul, made Elizabeth wish she had brought a fan with her tonight as her mother had suggested. It was no wonder Miss Bingley was so desperate to gain his favour, and, Elizabeth thought with a thrill of amusement, Miss Bingley was just the sort of lady to suit a self-important gentleman like Mr. Darcy.

"If you will excuse me," Mr. Bingley interrupted Elizabeth's thoughts just as she was deciding it would be an entertaining lark to match Mr. Darcy and Miss Bingley, "Miss Mary and I are needed for this next set."

"But Charles, I had hoped you would dance with me." Miss Bingley possessed a very pretty and practised pout.

"I am sorry, but I am not available." He sent a teasing look at his friend. "Darcy seems to be in want of a partner."

"I will not dance two sets with anyone," Darcy snapped.

"You are too fastidious," Bingley said with a laugh before turning to Mary and escorting her to the floor while leaving Elizabeth with his sisters and Mr. Darcy.

Elizabeth stood there for a long silent moment

before looking toward the door to her right. "I should go find my sisters."

"Sisters?" Darcy parroted.

"Yes, my sisters."

"How many do you have?" His eyes shifted from her to where his friend was preparing to dance with Mary.

She did not appreciate his shocked and demanding tone. No doubt he was finding fault in her family not having the prescribed number of daughters – whatever that number might be.

"Five," she replied. "There is Jane, then myself, then Mary, followed by Kitty and Lydia. How many do you have, sir?" She fluttered her lashes at him. Not because she was flirting with him, but because she found him annoying. Much to her delight he looked a trifle confused and taken aback at her reply and question.

"One," he said, followed by, "Have you any brothers?"

"No. Not a one."

"Indeed."

"And do you have any brothers, sir?"

"No. It is just my sister and I." His head tipped

as he looked at her with a puzzled expression. "This set has not yet started. Would you like to dance?"

So now he wanted to dance with her, did he? That was never going to happen! If he could not have been bothered to ask her to dance earlier, he did not deserve the privilege now. "I am afraid that is not possible."

"Why? Are you already engaged for this set?" His look of bewilderment deepened.

"No, but I do need to find my sisters, and, I find that I am in no humour at present to give consequence to gentlemen who slight ladies. You would do better to seek a dance with Miss Bingley, for, I fear, you are wasting your time with me."

The shock in his eyes caused her to smile broadly. "It was a pleasure to meet you, Miss Bingley and Mrs. Hurst. I am certain my mother would welcome a call." Dipping a curtsey, she added, "If you will excuse me," and took her leave.

Chapter 2

Of all the brash responses a lady might give a gentleman who had asked her to dance, Miss Elizabeth's must be amongst the brashest. Darcy should be furious at her for her insolence, and, to a degree, he was. However, he also found it strangely refreshing and very nearly humorous.

"I cannot imagine what she was thinking, refusing a man of Mr. Darcy's consequence," Louisa Hurst whispered very loudly to her sister.

While Mrs. Hurst might not be able to understand why Miss Elizabeth would refuse him, Darcy understood completely the reason for both why and how. Miss Elizabeth's reason was not hidden. Indeed, it stood forth boldly in the words she had used, for in her refusal, she had repeated word for word, with a few alterations to fit the context, the very words he had said to Bingley earlier tonight. He had not cared at the time if the lady whom Bingley was pointing out to him heard his cutting remarks. Now, however, having had his own rudeness thrown back at him, he felt the guilt he should have felt all along. While his words might have conveyed precisely and truthfully what he had felt in that moment when Bingley was pressing him to dance, they had been far from gentlemanly.

"What do you expect from country folk?" Caroline replied. "They are not so refined as the company in which we are used to finding ourselves. We must make allowances for their lack of breeding. One should not expect a sow to parade about the barnyard in fine feathers as a peacock does for a sow finds its home in the mud."

"Are you referring to your neighbours as livestock?" Darcy looked down his nose at Caroline. She was handsome and her dowry was noteworthy, but, at present, he found her arrogance excessively annoying. This, he supposed, was what Bingley had tried to tell him earlier this evening before they left Netherfield for the assembly. Caroline had attended the best schools, and she possessed the skills to be a fine manager of a grand home such as Pemberley, but her acerbic tongue did begin to grate on one's nerves at times.

Bingley was right. He should not consider Caroline as a wife. It had been a foolish notion. Instead, he must, as Bingley told him, consider not just the ability of a lady to manage a household or host a newsworthy soiree. He must also think about how many hours he would have to spend at home with such a woman. Darcy's houses were large, which gave ample space for he and his future wife to not be in contact with one another too often if necessary, but loneliness in marriage was far worse a thing than loneliness when one was actually alone.

"I am only attempting to make the analogy fit our surroundings."

Normally, Darcy might indulge in a chuckle at such a disparaging quip. Currently, however, he could not bring himself to do so, and he was not entirely sure why, though he suspected it was due to Miss Elizabeth's lesson in gentlemanly behaviour. Had any lady ever dared to instruct him on his behaviour? Again, he thought he should be put out with her, and he was. His pride stung and likely would for some time, but even so, he could not fault her completely.

"Your brother would like to make friends in the area. I do not think you are helping him do so if you are talking in such a fashion about his – and your – neighbours."

Caroline blinked and quickly hid her look of horror. "You cannot be thinking of encouraging him to take this estate permanently?"

"I have not been at Netherfield long enough to know whether I should encourage him or not."

"You must not," Louisa said. "A fashionable home in town and an estate near Pemberley is what he needs. He does not need to be here where there is such a want of refinement."

"Netherfield is close to town," Darcy offered. "And it is not completely abhorrent." Heat crept up his neck. He knew he was arguing where he had not before.

"Are you well? Did you contract some sort of

illness when travelling here from town?" Louisa asked, earning her a mild scold from her sister.

"His brain must be addled, Caroline, if he cannot see that this area is beneath Charles. Father did not leave our brother the fortune he did to have him use it to purchase an estate with no connections or hope of future connections that would lift him from where he is," Louisa continued. "I thought Mr. Darcy understood that. I dare say it is the foul air in the country that turns a man of sense into a gentleman who is lacking the proper use of his mental faculties."

"I promise you I am still in sound possession of my mental faculties. I am only attempting to view things from many vantage points. I would suggest that you do the same. Netherfield might be just what Bingley needs. It is a fine house, and the lands, while not extensive, are adequate for someone who is new to estate management."

Caroline looked perplexed. "I suppose," she said after a moment's consideration of what Darcy had said, "that, should Charles decide on Netherfield, he would become the highest-ranking gentleman in the area. I do not think there is any who has the fortune he does. He is already far superior to Mr. Bennet, and although, according to Sir William, Longbourn is the principal estate in the area –"

"Longbourn would still remain larger than Netherfield Park."

Caroline scowled at Darcy's interruption. "As I was saying, although Longbourn is the principal estate in the area, I hear that the income from it is not large. Would not Mr. Bennet's lower financial standing make Charles of greater importance?"

"To some," Darcy admitted.

There were those who judged a man purely upon what his coffers held and did not care a bit if the coffers were housed in a modest estate or a palace. Some required such a fellow to own at least a parcel of land, while others, such as his father, did not care if the fortune a man possessed came from warehouses and woolen mills.

"Your father wished for his son to own land so that he and his descendants would be considered gentlemen and gentlemen's daughters. Netherfield would give your brother that."

"But status is important," Louisa countered.

"I will not argue that any more than to say that Bingley's status will be secure as a gentleman no matter if he purchases Netherfield or some other estate."

From the small frown Louisa wore, Darcy knew his answer had not completely satisfied her. Thankfully, she did not deign to argue her point further.

"If you would excuse me, I think I would like to take a walk," Dary said.

"Oh, yes! A walk would be quite lovely, would it not be, Louisa?" Caroline wrapped her arm around Darcy's arm before it was even offered. "I have not gotten to dance and am feeling quite restless."

"I would not be opposed to doing something other than watching Charles prance about with every lady in attendance," Louisa grumbled. "I wish he were more like Mr. Darcy."

"I would not wish such a fate upon him," Darcy returned.

His friend met new acquaintances and formed attachments easily. Darcy, on the other hand, found it difficult to fit in with nearly everyone. Even some of his family found him odd. But no matter how frequently he attempted to exert himself, his nature simply would not allow him to be at ease until he knew someone quite well.

"It is a fate that would stand him in good stead," Louisa said.

Darcy knew that Louisa could be downright mulish at times, and tonight, seemed to be one of those times.

"Do you wish to take some air or find a cup of punch?" he asked.

"I think a cup of punch would be just the thing, and then, we can take some air," Caroline replied.

Darcy led them to the supper room and located a table at which they could sit before leaving them to procure the required beverage. There was somewhat of a crowd at the refreshment table, and people jostled each other as they moved in and out of line. With a sigh, Darcy settled into the mass of people that crawled forward slowly. He had hoped to find a quiet place to ponder a pretty pair of amber eyes and the fiery lady who possessed them.

Miss Elizabeth. He let the name roll around his mind as he wondered if she spoke to everyone as she had to him. It was not right for a lady to be so forward, he knew this, and yet, she piqued his interest. He should likely put her out of his mind. However, since he was only curious about her because she was a novelty and nothing more, he ignored the niggling feeling that he was treading where he should not and continued to ponder her

Engrossed in his contemplations, he allowed the crowd beside and behind him to guide his movement toward the table that held cups of punch. So it was that when Darcy saw, out the corner of his eye that the gentleman next to him was moving, Darcy also stepped forward just as the young lady in front of him turned from the table with a cup of punch in her hand.

The cold and sweet liquid in the young lady's glass sloshed and spilled as he plowed into her.

"Oh, I am dreadfully sorry," the young lady, who looked no older than his own sister, said before stopping a giggle by applying her fingers to her lips.

"No, no, I should have been paying closer attention to where I was going." That was not what he truly wanted to say, but he had already been called out for ungentlemanly behaviour by one young lady tonight so to rail at this clumsy child would not do. Instead, Darcy pulled his handkerchief from his pocket and began patting fiercely at his jacket while his stocking became more and more uncomfortably soggy.

"I truly am sorry, sir," the young lady repeated. "You may use my handkerchief if you would like."

"No, just be on your way." He closed his eyes and shook his head. "Thank you for your kind offer."

"Are you certain that we cannot help you in some way?"

Darcy's eyes sifted to the left. There was a second young lady standing just next to the first young lady and bearing very similar features. They must be sisters. Though he was certain he had never met either of them before, they both looked rather familiar.

"I do not see how you could," he replied as politely as possible. "I think you have done enough."

"I told you to be careful, Lydia," the second young lady grumbled to the first as the two moved away from Darcy just as a maid came bearing cloths to clean up the puddle of punch on the floor.

"Lydia?" Darcy murmured to himself.

"Yes, sir. Miss Lydia and Miss Kitty is their names. I can take you to their father if you wish to speak to him," the maid offered.

"Mr. Bennet?"

"Yes, sir. That be their father."

Ah. That explained why they looked so familiar. It appeared Miss Elizabeth had not found her sisters, for she did not seem to be with them.

"Do you want me to take you to their father?"

Darcy shook his head. "No, no. It was an accident."

"I would not be so sure," the maid muttered.

"Could you tell me if you saw any of their older sisters here?"

"Not for some time," the maid replied. "Was you looking for one in particular?" There was an interested glint in the maid's eye.

"No. I just heard Miss Elizabeth say she was going to find her sisters, and I was wondering if these were the sisters for whom she was looking and if she had found them."

"She's not found them if you be standing in soiled stockings," the maid replied. "Miss Elizabeth would have snatched them up if she saw you. She tries right hard to keep them from causing too much trouble, she does."

"She does?" Why was Miss Elizabeth tending to her sisters? Where were her mother and father? "Just Miss Elizabeth?"

The maid placed a final soiled towel in her basket. The floor was as dry as it could be. It would need a scrubbing, of course, but at least the threat of someone slipping on the liquid was gone.

"Miss Jane and Miss Mary help her, but Miss Lizzy is the sharpest with them."

That settled that. He was not the only person Miss Elizabeth felt a need to correct.

"Is she a harridan? I had not thought so when I met her."

"Miss Lizzy? A harridan?" the maid asked in surprise. "No, not at all. She just does not abide a fool as they say."

"I see. I am relieved to know I was not wrong in my assessment." But apparently, he was what Miss Elizabeth would call a fool for she had taken him to task.

"I should not say it, but you'd do well to call on her, sir."

Her words hit Darcy like a bucket of cold water to the face. "Oh, I am not planning on calling on anyone. I was merely curious about a new acquaintance."

"If you say so, sir." The maid offered him a towel. Then, she gave a curtsey before scurrying away wearing a sly grin.

Wonderful! Not only had he had his behaviour challenged by a young lady who likely thought him a fool. He had now started a rumor that he was interested in that same young woman.

He shook his head. He should have refused Bingley's invitation. Nothing good was going to come from him being somewhere he did not wish to be. He had known it when he received the invitation, but his sense of loyalty to a friend had required him to accept. Of all the stupid things to do!

Still remonstrating himself for his foolishness, he procured two cups of punch and headed back to the table where he had left Caroline and her sister.

Chapter 3

Elizabeth stood near the door to the courtyard. The coolness of the gentle breeze that wafted through the open door was refreshing.

"I hear that Mr. Darcy is inquiring after you." Charlotte Lucas, Elizabeth's dearest friend, hid her smile behind a glass of punch.

"I am certain you heard no such thing."

Charlotte's teasing about possible matches was not an unusual thing, for she was very marriage-minded. Not a day she and Elizabeth spent together went by without Charlotte making some mention of marriage. A bit of lace would be perfect to trim a cap. A delicious dish required the acquisition of the receipt for when she hosted a party. A gentleman was inspected with a practiced eye. His features would be declared acceptable or wanting. His income and property would be inquired after. To a point, Elizabeth could understand Charlotte's preoccupation with the marital state for Charlotte, at the age of twenty-seven, was in grave danger of being labeled a spinster.

"I assure you I did. I was at the refreshment table just now and heard Mr. Darcy asking the maid who was cleaning the floor about you." She took a sip of her punch. "He wanted to know if you were a harridan, though he had not thought you to be one when he met you."

Elizabeth gasped. "A harridan?" She knew she had been rather forward, but a harridan? *That* she was not!

Charlotte's eyebrows waggled. "I would like to know about that meeting. Securing him and his fortune would be quite the accomplishment, and it sounds as if you made quite the impression on him."

"I do not want either him or his fortune! He is rude." Handsome, but rude.

"I will allow that he thinks well of himself, but rude, Eliza?" Her head shook from side to side in disagreement. "I have not seen a single thing to indicate that Mr. Darcy is rude. A lady, such as yourself, must know that a gentleman of his wealth will be somewhat inclined to holding himself at a distance. As we both know, there are some women who find only those gentlemen with a handsome fortune to be to their liking and will do whatever is necessary to attain that fortune."

That was true. As Elizabeth had wandered the assembly, pretending to look for her sisters and to avoid dancing with Mr. Darcy, she had heard the whispers of more than one mother as they discussed Mr. Bingley and his friend. They had made little mention of anything about the gentleman other than their income. While Mr. Darcy's manners had done little to recommend him to these ladies, they would happily overlook such a flaw to acquire his ten thousand a year. Even she had to admit that such a sum was impressive, but, to her, it was not so impressive that it could make up for his ungentlemanly behaviour.

Charlotte was looking at her expectantly. Apparently, silently allowing what Charlotte had said to be true was not going to be enough for her friend to end their discussion of Mr. Darcy.

"He has been barely civil all evening," Elizabeth replied, "and he said something very unkind about me."

Charlotte leaned toward Elizabeth. "What did he say?"

Elizabeth took a quick glance around her to see if anyone was close enough to hear her before answering. "He said that I was tolerable but not handsome enough to tempt him into dancing with me, and even if I had been handsome enough for the likes of him. And do you know why? He would not have considered me since I was sitting and not dancing, and, therefore, he believed me to be slighted by other gentlemen, which means I must be lacking in more than beauty." His comments, as she replayed them in her mind, still cut deeply.

"I cannot believe it. Surely, he was speaking about someone else."

Elizabeth shook her head. "I assure you he was not. He looked right at me before saying what he did, and, while that gives his remarks a depth of rudeness that is excessively intolerable, it truly does not matter if he was speaking about me or someone else. His words were reprehensible."

Her friend's eyebrows were lifted high. "I truly cannot believe him to be so unfeeling. He did not present himself to be so when I met him. He was reserved but proper." She paused. "And he did not raise his voice at Lydia or seek out your father when Lydia spilled her punch on him."

Elizabeth's hand flew to her heart. "What did Lydia do?" Oh, she knew she should have gone in search of her youngest sister in earnest rather than seeking what peace she could find to reflect on the events of the evening.

"She was not watching where she was going and turned right into him, spilling nearly all of her punch on him."

Elizabeth closed her eyes. "How bad was it?"

"He was drying his jacket with his handkerchief while speaking to the maid, who was wiping up the puddle at his feet."

"Was it just his jacket which was damaged?"

Charlotte shook her head. "His stockings and

shoes seemed to have also fallen victim to the collision." She took another sip of her punch. "He was actually very gracious to Lydia."

"Did she apologize?"

Charlotte nodded. "With a giggle."

It was as Elizabeth feared, Lydia knew what she had done was wrong, yet she could not ignore the humor in her own folly. Elizabeth sighed. "I suppose I should go find her."

"I will go with you. I believe she and Kitty are with Maria." Charlotte placed her empty glass on a table near the door to the courtyard. "Jane seems to have made a favourable impression on Mr. Bingley."

"Indeed, she has, and I, for one, could not be more pleased."

"Do you think she admires him as much as he so obviously admires her?"

"Have you not seen her smiles?"

"Jane smiles all the time."

"But not as she is tonight. I dare say she is half in love with him already, and they have only danced twice." She grasped Charlotte's arm excitedly. "Twice. He danced with her twice, and he said that he told his friend that he would dance a third with her if there was a third to be had."

"He did not!"

"He did, and while he admitted to me it was said to provoke his friend, he also admitted that it was not void of desire. He likes Jane very much, Charlotte."

"I am delighted to hear it even if I am a trifle jealous." Her friend sighed. "Mr. Reed has yet to dance more than one set with me. I have been as patient as I can be, but I fear it is time to once again give up hope."

"Oh, Charlotte." Elizabeth squeezed her friend's arm tightly. "Do not give up hope just yet. Is it not you who constantly reminds me that a man must be enticed and that a lady's aspirations must be presented clearly?"

"I do not know what else to do, Elizabeth. I have been as attentive and charming as I am capable of being."

"Have you sought him out, and I do not mean at an assembly, but at church or just on the street in Meryton?"

Charlotte nodded. "I must face the reality of life. I shall be fortunate to receive an offer from any gentleman."

"I refuse to believe it. I just know that there must be a gentleman of sense who can see you for the wonderful person you are."

"As much as I wish for you to be correct, I fear that should I ever be fortunate enough to receive an offer, I shall have to accept it no matter who the fellow is, provided, of course, that the gentleman has a reasonable income and situation. My days of romantic notions are at an end."

"Do not say so." It hurt Elizabeth's heart to hear the dejection in her friend's tone.

"I have accepted it – mostly," Charlotte said with a small sad smile. "I will not give up my pursuit of Mr. Reed completely until I must. However, I shall turn my romantic fancies to helping my friends find gentlemen to adore them."

"You will have a hard time finding any such gentleman for me. I am far too outspoken."

"I will not disagree with that! But..." She glanced to her left and then her right before whispering, "There is Mr. Darcy, and he was inquiring after you."

"No. He will not do." She leaned her head closer to Charlotte. "I think he would do well with Miss Bingley. She certainly seems to admire him, and her hauteur would match well with his offensiveness."

Charlotte's brow furrowed, and she grimaced. "I do not think that is a good match at all. He is good friends with Mr. Bingley, and there must be a reason that two such different personalities find companionability in each other."

"It is because Mr. Bingley likely wishes to settle his sister at Mr. Darcy's estate – what was it called?"

"Pemberley?"

"Yes. Pemberley."

"Elizabeth Bennet, you are the most foolish young woman I have the pleasure of calling my friend."

Elizabeth rolled her eyes. That was Charlotte's way of saying Elizabeth was wrong.

"Mr. Darcy needs a lively wife, someone who smiles and teases and occasionally taunts. I would venture to guess that Mr. Bingley and Mr. Darcy's relationship works because they balance each other. It is much like you and me. We are very different, yet we work well together."

Her reasoning was not without sense, which was annoying.

"To approach it from a different point of view. Do you see our sisters?" Charlotte asked

Kitty, Lydia, and Maria were just in front of them, whispering and giggling together.

"That is what happens when personalities that are too similar are put together. It is not a good thing. While it is tolerable in friends, especially young ones who have yet to find their footing on their own, it would be disastrous in a marriage. Mr. Darcy and Miss Bingley would not be a good pairing."

Elizabeth smiled as she saw her opportunity to prove Charlotte wrong. "What about Mr. Bingley and Jane? Are they not similar? Should we not encourage them? Perhaps we should attempt to tear them apart!"

Charlotte wore a look that said Elizabeth was being ridiculous. "Jane is calm. Mr. Bingley is more exuberant. I think that is a difference enough for them to find happiness."

Elizabeth sighed. It was nearly impossible to win an argument with Charlotte when she was set in her thinking as she seemed to be on this. Of course, that did not mean Elizabeth would simply accept what her friend said was true.

"Believe what you will. I am going to encourage the match."

Charlotte laughed. "You will find I am right, but I will not stop you."

Elizabeth stopped walking, though they were only two steps away from their sisters. Charlotte was being too agreeable. She was supposed to tell Elizabeth how she was wasting her time and attempt to persuade her from her course of action.

"Why?"

"Why what?" Charlotte's tone was far too innocent-sounding.

"Why will you not stop me?"

"Do you wish for me to stop you?"

"No, but usually, when I tell you I am going to

do something you think is wrong, you attempt to stop me."

Her friend's lips tipped into a satisfied smile. "Your plan works to my advantage."

"Charlotte, you are making no sense."

She shrugged. "You will eventually see." She closed the distance between them and their sisters, effectively cutting off the discussion.

"I heard you met Mr. Darcy," Charlotte said to Lydia.

"Not officially. We have not been introduced," Lydia replied before sighing loudly. "Is he not the handsomest gentleman ever?"

"I would not disagree that he is handsome," Charlotte replied. "Would you disagree, Elizabeth?"

"A handsome face fades in its attractiveness when the ugliness of a gentleman's character is put on display."

Lydia sucked in a breath, and her eyes grew wide.

"It is true," Elizabeth protested.

"It is," a deep voice behind her said. "I know several gentlemen and ladies who appear to be far more agreeable than their natures actually are."

Slowly, with her heart hammering within her chest and mortification twisting her stomach, Elizabeth turned toward the gentleman about whom they had been speaking. "Mr. Darcy," she greeted with a curtsey. "Have you met my sisters and my friends?"

"I have been introduced to the Miss Lucases, and I have met your sisters, though we have not been introduced."

For a moment, Elizabeth was at a loss as to what she should say for Mr. Darcy was smiling, and it was a perfectly agreeable smile that set off his features quite nicely. She pulled her eyes away from his face and noticed the stain on his jacket. Then, her eyes dropped to his legs. His calves were... well, clad in soiled stockings and yet very attractive.

"Mr. Darcy," Charlotte intervened, "allow me to present to you Miss Lydia and Miss Kitty Bennet. Lydia, Kitty, this is Mr. Fitzwilliam Darcy of Pemberley in Derbyshire."

Elizabeth's cheeks were burning. When had

she been so distracted by a gentleman's appearance that she forgot what she was doing? Never, that's when. Never. Until now.

"Ladies, it is a pleasure to meet you."

"We are dreadfully sorry about the punch," Kitty said.

"As I said before, I also should have been paying better attention to my surroundings." He turned his attention to Elizabeth. "I am happy to see you have finally found your sisters."

"Was Lizzy looking for us?" Lydia asked.

"She said she was."

"Indeed? How odd."

"It is not odd," Elizabeth protested. "I like to know where you are and what you are doing because when I do not..." She glanced at Mr. Darcy, who seemed to be smirking – the infuriating man! "A gentleman ends up wearing punch," she concluded.

"We really are sorry," Kitty repeated.

Elizabeth folded her arms and looked at Lydia. "Are you truly?"

Lydia nodded. "We are."

The reply would have held more weight if

Lydia did not look as if she were fighting to contain a giggle, and were Mr. Darcy not standing behind her, Elizabeth would have confronted Lydia regarding her amused appearance. However, as it was, there was no need for that gentleman to hear such a speech, for it would likely only give him more reasons to find her unacceptable. She clenched her teeth. How foolish was she being? Why should she care at all whether or not he approved of her?

"Now that you have found your sisters," Mr. Darcy said, interrupting Elizabeth's admonishment of herself, "and can see that they are well, will you still refuse to dance with me?"

Elizabeth's eyes grew wide as Lydia gasped and then loudly whispered, "You refused to dance with him?"

"Yes, she did," Mr. Darcy replied while Elizabeth wished to sink into the floor. Lydia would tell their mother and then there would be a great long and loud lecture to endure.

There was nothing to do but paste a pleasant expression on her face and...

"Charlotte, would you be so kind as to keep

an eye on my troublesome sisters while I dance with Mr. Darcy?" That should help somewhat when it came to her mother's displeasure. She had no doubt she would still have to endure a lecture, but dancing with Mr. Darcy should help curtail the length of her mother's reproof.

"We are not troublesome," Lydia protested.

Elizabeth's eyebrows rose over a pointed look which she directed at her youngest sister before shifting her gaze to Mr. Darcy and then back to her sister. "I believe Mr. Darcy's jacket agrees with my assessment."

Lydia had the good sense to look somewhat contrite and hold her tongue.

"I would be delighted to spend some time with our sisters," Charlotte said. "Quite delighted."

From her friend's eager smile and tone, Elizabeth knew that Charlotte would have much to say about this later.

"Miss Elizabeth," Mr. Darcy held his hand out to her, and, reluctantly, she placed her hand in his.

Chapter 4

As soon as Miss Elizabeth's hand landed lightly in his, Darcy knew that the niggling feeling, which whispered to him that it was a mistake to ask her to dance in such a fashion as left her little room to refuse, had been speaking the truth. Blast his pride for insisting that he not be refused by a simple country girl! Simple country girl indeed! She was far from simple as he had witnessed in her first refusal. He might have thought his decision to seek her out was based on a need to put her in her place, but the fizz of whatever that was which danced up his arm at her touch told him it was his desire and not his pride which had led him to where he was at present.

"Are you certain you wish to be seen by one and all dressed as you are?" Miss Elizabeth asked.

"Are you attempting to withdraw your acceptance?" At present, he would allow her to do so just so his insides could stop their quivering. He had never enjoyed being put on display in a new environment, and he knew that very few would not take notice of his dancing with one of their own, especially when he had danced with no other lady from the area all night. His chest constricted. Asking Miss Elizabeth to dance had most certainly been a mistake.

"Of course not," she replied. "I was only thinking of your comfort."

One of Darcy's eyebrows quirked of its own accord. Her tone was far too cajoling. "Indeed?" And now her lips were doing their tempting best to not smile.

"Indeed. I imagine that to have tongues wag over one's soiled attire will not be comfortable."

She had a point. He was not just dancing with a new acquaintance – one who had refused him at first – His head tipped as that fact arrested whatever other thought he might have had.

"They will not only be whispering about me," he said.

"Oh, I dare say they will not be," she answered readily. "Only think of it. A lady such as me being asked to dance by someone of your consequence. It really should not be, should it?" Her words dripped with disdain.

"I apologize for my ill manners, but I was not speaking about that."

"Were you not?"

They had drawn to a stop at the edge of the ballroom.

"No. If you will remember, you refused to dance with me when I first asked. I am certain the gossips will find that bit of information interesting enough to discuss."

She gasped. "How would they even know that I refused you?"

His lips tipped into a smile. "It has been my experience, gained through my association with Bingley and his sisters, that it takes very few knowing about some bit of interesting news before that morsel of news becomes the talk of the assembly. Even now, your sisters or the Miss Lucases might be sharing your refusal with someone."

Next to him, Miss Elizabeth seemed to be struggling to keep her composure. He was almost certain she was going to say something sharp to him, and part of him was eager to hear what her jibe would be. However, he was to be disappointed, for she turned the subject of their discussion in an unexpected direction.

"Miss Bingley dances very well."

He eyed her warily. "She does. She was instructed by some of the best masters."

"I was not. It will be quite a disappointment to you to have to dance with me when you could be dancing this set with Miss Bingley."

"I doubt you will disappoint."

"I can assure you I might. Would it not be better if I were to fetch Miss Bingley to take my place?"

"Ah-ha! You *are* attempting to withdraw your acceptance."

She scowled. "I am not! I am once again thinking of your comfort."

"I doubt that very much, Miss Elizabeth."

"Just because you do not think a thing is true does not mean it is false." Her chin lifted, and her eyes did that wonderful flashing thing they had done before when she had refused him. She was fury fetchingly personified. "Do you like having your toes trampled upon, Mr. Darcy?"

"It would not be the first time I have endured such treatment. My sister was not so quick a study of dance as she was of playing the piano." That seemed to momentarily befuddle her. But only momentarily.

"Did your sister step on your toes while you were at an assembly?"

"Georgiana is not yet out, so how could it have been at an assembly?"

That caused her to smile somewhat triumphantly, and he recognized her plan of attack.

"But," he added quickly, "I would gladly endure sore toes and damaged shoes for her pleasure even at an assembly."

"But that is because she is your sister," Miss Elizabeth retorted with some force.

This was perhaps the most enjoyment Darcy had ever found at a ball.

"Do you think it is impossible for me to take pleasure in dancing with you?" That was more forward than he had ever been with any lady. Ever. And while his features might not have registered his unease with being so forward, his ears warmed quite nicely at his words.

Miss Elizabeth looked at him in utter disbelief. "With me? A lady who is merely tolerable and slighted by other gentlemen? You expect me to believe that you would find pleasure in dancing with such a lady as me?"

An older lady to Elizabeth's right glanced at him. Their conversation was not going unnoticed.

"I have already apologized for my poor manners."

"But you have not apologized for your words, sir." She turned away from him. "And now, you attempt to make a fool of me for whatever sport you can find in it."

"No!" The word was out of his mouth nearly before it had passed through his mind. "My words were a part of my manners. Neither were acceptable. You were right to chastise me for my actions – and my words. Shall we?" He motioned to the floor that was in the midst of transition from being filled with those who had danced to those who were about to dance.

"I suppose we must. However, I will remind you that the fault for the fate of your toes is yours alone because I have warned you."

Her jaw was set firmly, and she barely spared him a glance. If he was guessing correctly, which he did not always do when attempting to decipher what a lady was thinking, he would have to say that Miss Elizabeth was more than angry for how he had spoken earlier. She was also hurt. Such knowledge sat even worse with him than knowing he had angered her.

"I truly am sorry," he said as they took their places.

Her response was a small incline of her head, but he did not believe for one moment that it meant he was forgiven.

"Mr. Bingley was not limping after dancing with you," he said to her as the music began, "I dare say you do not pose a threat to my toes at all."

She arched an eyebrow at him. "But surely

there must have been a reason I was being slighted."

He shook his head.

She batted her lashes, an action that seemed very out of place for her. "And I quite like Mr. Bingley. He is all that is pleasant."

"Unless you do not wish to do as he suggests," Darcy muttered, causing Miss Elizabeth to nearly laugh. How he would have loved to hear her laugh! He was certain just from how infectious her smile was that her laugh must also fill those around her with mirth.

"Am I to believe, then, that Mr. Bingley is sometimes unpleasant?" she asked when they joined hands for a turn.

"Yes, for it is the truth." They parted for a few beats of music and then returned to each other.

"Is he unpleasant with everyone or just you?" Her look was one of sheer impertinence.

Darcy could not help but chuckle which seemed to cause Miss Elizabeth to stumble and one dainty foot fell with a good deal of force on his foot. Darcy caught her by the arm and kept her from any further missteps.

"I do apologize," she said.

Her cheeks were emblazoned with her embarrassment. Her eyes did not seem to wish to leave him, but after a moment or two of observation, she turned away. It was a pity. Her expressive eyes were perhaps her most enchanting feature. Not that she was devoid of charm save for her eyes. Not at all.

He had been lying quite blatantly when he said she was not handsome or tempting. She was both, though not as some might see it. She was no classic beauty. She would not be ranked as an incomparable in town. In fact, she would likely be passed over by many gentlemen for not being tall enough or willowy enough or blonde enough or some other foolish standard.

However, Darcy had never been one to agree with what was the current standard for beauty. He did not care what other men preferred. He wanted more than a pretty face with a pleasant smile who carried herself with a great deal of grace and elegance but no more than a hint of passion for anything. Miss Elizabeth seemed to have a deep storehouse of passion, and her eyes were the windows to such delights as might be had, no matter what the emotion, which she felt, was.

Yes, Darcy admitted to himself, asking her to dance had been a mistake of epic proportions, for it had given him the opportunity to see her more clearly, and what he saw, he liked very much.

"Do you like books?" he asked when they had once again joined hands.

Her silence since her stumble compelled him to say something. He was not, however, very good at small talk. Still, he must make an attempt for her sake as it was definitely not for his own. He would normally like nothing better than to dance in silence. But not with her.

"They are very wonderful inventions," she replied with a flutter of lashes.

Was she flirting with him, or was she teasing him out of continued disdain? Choosing to err on the side of what he wished, he replied lightly. "Do you enjoy reading these creations of leather, paper, and ink?"

Ah, a smile. A pleasantly amused smile that curled her lips and shone in her eyes.

"Even more than I like dancing."

The music was coming to an end, and Darcy prepared to bow.

"I should like to say I never stumble when reading, but I have walked into a wall or two or taken a path that led me in the direction opposite of which I wished to go while reading."

"You do not sit and read?" How unusual.

Her eyebrows arched, and he, noting his surroundings, bowed, though belatedly.

"I am capable of reading in many attitudes. Sitting, lying down, standing, and walking." Her lips pursed in barely restrained amusement as she placed her hand in his and prepared to leave the dance floor. "I have even read in a carriage – while it was moving."

"It was not that odd a question," he grumbled. "Most people do not wander their homes and beyond while reading."

"I, sir, am not most people."

"So I have noticed," he replied. "Most ladies

would not have refused my first offer to dance. Most would have been angling to get an offer."

And most ladies did not interest him nearly as much as she did. Why had he asked her to dance? He should have felt the sting of her words and ignored the curiosity she aroused in him. It would have been safer. Safer, but not as enjoyable.

"You are so well-liked as that, then?"

He could well understand the surprise in her voice. He knew he was not the most-friendly looking fellow when in a ballroom. It was both naturally and purposefully done.

"No," he admitted, "but my estate and wealth are. I am merely the means to a desired end."

From the wideness of her eyes and the way she blinked, he had surprised her as much as he had surprised himself with such an admission. He was not one to share such things with anyone except his nearest and dearest friends, and even then, it would only be done once half-foxed. She was intoxicatingly dangerous.

"I thank you for the honor of a dance," he said with a bow when he returned her to where the Miss Lucases and the younger Miss Bennets were standing at the side of the ballroom. "Now, if you will excuse me, I shall see myself home to find a fresh set of clothing." And give himself a stern lecture about pride and the beautiful temptation, named Miss Elizabeth Bennet, to which it had led.

"Will you call on us?" Miss Lydia inquired before he could move more than two steps away.

"If my friend is calling at Longbourn, I shall join him." Her smile told him that his answer was welcomed by her, while the scowl on her elder sister's face made him question just how welcomed he would be.

Be that as it may, he would call if Bingley did, and he would find another time to speak to Miss Elizabeth. For, though he had snubbed others without care, none of them had accused him of being ungentlemanly, and he must, simply must, demonstrate to the lovely Miss Elizabeth that he was nothing if not a gentleman.

Chapter 5

"He is here! He is here!" Lydia fairly danced into the drawing room at Longbourn the next day, crossing very quickly from the door to the windows that faced the front courtyard with Kitty following close behind.

"Who is here?" Mrs. Bennet demanded.

"Mr. Bingley," Kitty answered.

"And Mr. Dar-cy." Lydia turned fluttery eyes at Elizabeth as she said the gentleman's name in a sing-song tone.

Elizabeth rolled her eyes at her sister but refrained from saying anything to her. It had been at least an hour since their mother had last muttered something about obstinate girls being spinsters, and Elizabeth had no desire to open that discussion once again, especially as the man was nearly on their doorstep. She glanced at the door.

"Do not think of running away, Lizzy," Lydia said with a laugh.

"I was not thinking of running away." Her protest was patently false. She had hoped to perhaps make an escape before their mother's attention could be turned in her direction.

Mrs. Bennet rose from where she had been pushing her workbasket under her chair and looked at her second eldest daughter with one of her infrequently used, but very effective, stern glares.

"You will be polite. Ten thousand a year is nothing to be shunned." Her mother's lips pursed. "Even if he did not declare you handsome immediately, he did seem to come to his senses." She shook her head as if bewildered. How many times since they had arrived home last night after the assembly had she muttered, "tolerable?" or "not handsome enough?" in a tone of utter unbelief?

Elizabeth sighed. It had been equal to the number of times that Elizabeth had been reprimanded for refusing a gentleman worth ten thousand a year.

"Not everyone can be as clever as Mr. Bingley," Mrs. Bennet added with a smile.

"That is because Jane is beautiful."

Mrs. Bennet arched an eyebrow at Elizabeth. "You are no sow's snout. Straighten your lace."

There was nothing wrong with the lace at Elizabeth's collar, but Elizabeth straightened it anyway. When their mother used the tone she had just used, one did not push back. There were limits to Mrs. Bennet's indulgence and refusing a wealthy gentleman a dance or suggesting that one of her daughters was not worthy to be painted by the masters due to her beauty were immovable boundaries that were not crossed without some threat of punishment. Not even Lydia was allowed to breach those bounds.

Mrs. Bennet came to stand in front of Elizabeth just as a knock at the front door could be heard. "Your book." She extended her hand.

"Mama, I will be welcoming."

"Yes, I know you will be. Now, give me your book. You may have it back once our guests have left and you have demonstrated how welcoming you can be."

Elizabeth did as she was told and placed the book in her mother's hand.

"Refusing a gentleman of Mr. Darcy's status," she muttered as she scooted across the room to tuck the book under her chair with the work-basket. She was just standing and smoothing her skirts when their visitors were announced.

Relief washed over Elizabeth when she saw that it was not just Mr. Bingley and Mr. Darcy who had come to call but also Miss Bingley.

"Miss Bingley, your dress is so beautiful," Elizabeth said as soon as her mother was done with her greetings. "You must come and tell me where you found such wonderful material." She motioned to the seat on the sofa next to where she was sitting. "Lydia come join us."

Lydia's mouth popped open and then closed again. "But Mr. –"

"Join us," Elizabeth said cutting off her youngest sister's protest.

"I thought you liked to read," Lydia muttered as she joined Elizabeth and Miss Bingley.

"I do, and Papa has many more books. I do not need that one." She smiled when she noticed that her exchange with her sister was not going unnoticed.

Miss Bingley darted a look between the two of them, and her brow furrowed.

"Lydia prefers the colours of autumn, and I think this shade of green would please her immensely," Elizabeth offered by way of explanation. It had nothing to do with what had caused Miss Bingley's brow to furrow, but there was no way Elizabeth was going to broach that subject.

"Do you not think it is a perfect shade?" she asked Lydia.

"I find it very lovely."

"And you Mr. Darcy," Elizabeth turned toward him as he had taken a seat close to where she was, but on her left, "do you not find this a charming colour?"

"I suppose I do." He looked a bit wary of answering which made Elizabeth wish to giggle.

"It is a very becoming shade on Miss Bingley, is it not?" she continued, pressing her lips together when the man shifted in his chair before agreeing that it was.

"And that is why I simply must know where you found such a wonderful fabric," Elizabeth effused.

"You must?" Lydia was looking excessively perplexed.

"Yes, I must."

Miss Bingley smoothed a hand over her skirt. "My modiste acquired it, so I am afraid I must disappoint you, for I do not know where it was found."

"Uncle Gardiner might know," Lydia suggested. "But, do you think it would look good on you? I should think it is too yellowy a colour for your complexion."

"It most certainly is, but it would not be for yours. I am certain of it." Elizabeth sighed as if disappointed for it seemed like the thing to do if one was truly interested in something. "However, my sense of fashion is not so good as yours or quite obviously, Miss Bingley's is."

She dared to peek at Mr. Darcy to see if he was listening. "Alas, that is likely because I am not a society lady. Jane and I do go to town on a regular basis to visit our relations, but they do not circulate in the upper circles."

"At least, you get to go to town," Lydia grumbled. "How I should love to see the shops and walk in the gardens!"

"You have relations in town?" Mr. Darcy asked.

Ah, how fortunate! This was just the opportunity Elizabeth needed to prove she was not the sort of lady upon whom he should bestow his attention.

"Yes, my mother's brother and his wife live near Cheapside. They have a lovely home on Gracechurch Street from which you can see my uncle's warehouses."

"Warehouses?" Miss Bingley said in surprise.

"Your uncle is in trade?" Mr. Darcy asked.

"He is."

"So, too, was my father," Bingley inserted. "That is how the late Mr. Darcy came to know him – through a business venture." He smiled. "Which, I might add, was very successful."

"Yes, father was very clever," Miss Bingley agreed, if somewhat reluctantly.

"I suppose I had heard that your father was in trade," Elizabeth said to Miss Bingley. How had she forgotten that? *I was a foolish oversight.*

"But I never would have guessed it from how elegant you are." She added a sigh of admiration for effect.

Miss Bingley smiled. "Thank you. I have been educated at the finest schools."

"That must be why you carry yourself so well." Then she added in a whisper that she hoped was loud enough for Mr. Darcy to hear. "I have not even attended one school. In fact, we never even had a governess. However, Mama and Papa have done their best to ensure we are not intolerably stupid."

Mr. Darcy coughed, drawing Elizabeth's attention. His eyes held amusement.

Good! Let him laugh at her so long as he took himself away and did not return.

"Many children are educated at home to no ill effect," he said once his coughing had subsided, and he had assured Mrs. Bennet that he was not in need of anything.

"You are very agreeable today," Elizabeth muttered before she could think better of it.

"I often am, am I not, Miss Bingley?" His left eyebrow arched in challenge.

"Oh, nearly always," Miss Bingley agreed with alacrity.

As Elizabeth attempted to keep from scowling at Mr. Darcy, the door to the drawing room opened.

"Mr. Newell, ma'am," Hill introduced the handsome gentleman behind her.

"Mr. Newell!" Mrs. Bennet cried. "What brings you to Longbourn?"

"My father would never hear of my not stopping to visit you on my way home. I dare say if I returned home without a report of how everyone gets on at Longbourn, he would turn me out until I had such a report to give him."

"Oh," Mrs. Bennet giggled and waved his words away.

"I also had some business with Philips," Mr. Newell added, with a quick survey of the room and a smile. "I had heard Mr. Bingley had taken Netherfield." He bowed to Mr. Bingley and then Miss Bingley. "Miss Bingley, you look fetching today, as always."

"You know Mr. Bingley and Miss Bingley?" Elizabeth asked.

"I do. We have met a time or six in town. I believe the last time was at a soiree where I had the pleasure of hearing Miss Bingley sing."

"You sing?" Elizabeth asked as she took note of how Miss Bingley's features were suffused with pleasure at Mr. Newell's words.

"I do."

"Nearly as well as you do, Miss Elizabeth."

"This is *that* Miss Elizabeth?" Miss Bingley cried.

Mr. Newell nodded. "It is indeed."

"Oh, how pleasant," Miss Bingley said, and she truly did look delighted to learn such information.

"Do you know Mr. Darcy?" was all that Elizabeth could think of to say.

"By sight and reputation, but I must say I have not yet had the pleasure to meet him." Mr.

Newell's eyes flicked momentarily from Elizabeth to Mr. Darcy before returning to her and waiting expectantly.

"Mr. Darcy, may I present a good friend of our family for many years, Mr. Simon Newell of Windham Manor in Bedfordshire. Mr. Newell, this is our new acquaintance of one day, Mr. Darcy of Pemberley in Derbyshire."

This, of course, was followed by all the pleasantries that would normally follow an introduction.

"Papa is not here," Lydia, who had abandoned her seat to Mr. Newell, said.

"I know. I saw both him and Sir William at Philips."

"Did he offer you a bed to sleep in?" Mrs. Bennet asked.

"He did, and I have informed Hill that I will be staying."

"Very good. You will have the same room as always."

There was not much that Elizabeth's mother liked more than entertaining, whether it be hosting just one guest or presiding over a dinner party of twenty-four.

"I am happy to hear it. I had considered just pressing on to home, but your husband would not hear of it. And," he cast a look at Elizabeth, "there are friends with whom I wish to reacquaint myself."

Elizabeth's cheeks warmed at the comment. Without his look in her direction, she would have known he meant her. Simon was a dear friend and as handsome as any gentleman could hope to be. She pulled the corner of her bottom lip between her teeth. Well, perhaps not so handsome as Mr. Darcy, but at least as handsome as Mr. Bingley, just with darker hair and green eyes. He was also just as amiable as Mr. Bingley, but he was Simon, and try as she might, Elizabeth could not think of him as anything but a friend.

"I am sorry I missed the assembly last night," Simon said. "Was it a success?"

"Oh, it was!" Mrs. Bennet cried. "Such a crush as I have never seen, but then, you know how it is when there are new neighbours to greet."

Simon laughed. "I do, indeed. My condo-lences," he said with a somber bow of his head to Bingley.

"No need to be uneasy on my part," Bingley said. "I quite enjoy a good crowd, and it did allow me to dance with the prettiest lady in all of Hertfordshire."

Jane blushed while Simon chuckled.

"I take it you danced with Miss Elizabeth, then?"

Elizabeth gasped. "He was speaking of Jane as you well know."

"Do I?" Simon teased.

"Yes, you do."

"Then, you did not get to dance with Mr. Bin-gley?"

"That is not what I said."

"So then, he did dance with the prettiest lady in Hertfordshire."

"And he also danced with me."

He was impossible. Simply impossible. Now was not an acceptable time to tease. They had guests, and it was making her feel very self-con-scious. He was a lot like her father in that way.

Elizabeth enjoyed her father's teasing to a point, but Simon went beyond that point quite often. Perhaps this was the true reason why she could not think of him as anything more than just Simon.

Simon chuckled. "Very well, we shall allow your sister to be the most beautiful, though I dare say it is hard to pick the prettiest gem out of a collection of precious stones, and each will have their preference and declare it the best. Is that not how it goes?"

"Yes. I suppose it does."

"So few words? Are you well?"

"Perfectly well. Are you certain you do not wish to sleep in your own bed tonight?" She would gladly walk him to his carriage and wave as he drove through the gate if it meant he would stop teasing her in front of everyone.

"Ah, I have gone too far," he said with a nod of his head.

"Yes, you have."

"Will you allow me to escort you on a turn of the garden if that would be acceptable to your mother?"

"Mary, go get your things and Elizabeth's," Mrs. Bennet said.

"But what of our guests," Mary asked.

"They may either stay here and continue chatting, or they can join you in the garden." She looked around the room. "I must agree it is a pleasant day."

"Why do we not all go for a walk?" Jane said.

"Capital idea!" Bingley agreed. "I do enjoy walking."

He likely enjoyed anything that was not sitting still, Elizabeth thought, for he seemed to overflow with energy.

"What do you say, Darcy?" Bingley asked.

"I am as fond of getting air as the next fellow."

So, it was decided that the whole party would take at least one turn of Longbourn's gardens.

Chapter 6

Darcy reined in his mount so that he could take in the view before him. The ground rose and fell in gentle swells and small undulations. There were stands of trees that interrupted fields and stood in both great and small gatherings. The countryside was beautiful but lacked the sharp edges that surrounded his home, which was utterly unfortunate, for, he thought to himself, a good rocky crag right in the middle of Longbourn's garden would have come in handy yesterday for disposing of the insufferable Mr. Newell. That man would not allow himself to be separated from the side of Miss Elizabeth. Not that Miss Bingley would have allowed Darcy to leave her side either.

Vexing botherations, the two of them! How was he supposed to prove to Miss Elizabeth that he was a gentlemanly sort of gentleman if he was separated from her at every turn.

His horse blew through its lips and shifted under him.

"My thoughts exactly, Aegeus. It is unsettling and frustrating business." Darcy nudged the beast's sides with his boots. "Go on. Take me up to the crest."

Immediately, his horse began walking up the well-worn trail they were on. There was most likely a very good vantage point from which to take in the area at the top of this rise for this path to be so worn – or, at least, Darcy hoped there was for that was why he was on his way up this hill. He wanted to get a good look at the place Bingley had chosen to call home.

Darcy had passed through this county a great number of times in his travels, but he had never taken the time to survey his surroundings. There had been no need to do so. He only needed to know the road and the inns. But now, he had a friend who was looking to him for advice, and so, he would do his duty and make his assessment as best he could.

If only women were as easy to read as the lay of the land and possibility of productive fields and the prosperity of a neighborhood were.

Darcy huffed in frustration as his thoughts turned back to Miss Elizabeth. Not only had Miss Bingley and Mr. Newell placed themselves in his path, the lady herself had done an admirable job of creating a separation. He was certain that Miss Elizabeth was not the sort of lady to coo over dresses and fripperies – or at least, he imagined she was not – and from the way her punch-spilling youngest sister had looked both shocked and confused when Miss Elizabeth began to talk about such things, Darcy thought it safe to assume his supposition was correct.

"Why Miss Bingley? Of all people," he said to the morning breeze. Caroline was fond enough of him and his estate without his being forced to compliment her on her appearance. She needed no encouragement!

Thanks to his call at Longbourn, he had been compelled to seek solitude in his bedchamber for so much of the evening as he could without being thought excessively rude. Bingley had, of course, found that fact nearly as amusing as he had found Darcy's attire at the end of the assembly two days ago.

Reaching the top of the hill, Darcy dismounted, secured his horse, and made his way toward where he imagined the best viewpoint would be. "I should just return to London," he said once again in conversation with the solitude of the morning as he straightened one of his gloves.

"It might be best if you are unhappy with where you are."

Darcy stopped walking and ignored the urge to straighten his other glove. Solitude was not supposed to reply. Slowly, he turned toward the source of the retort.

"Good morning, Mr. Darcy."

He should have been paying closer attention to his surroundings. How had he missed seeing the beguiling lady who greeted him.

"And good morning to you as well, Miss Elizabeth." He sketched a shallow bow. "I was hoping that this prominence would give me an excellent perspective from which to view the area."

Miss Elizabeth returned to her seat on a log which seemed hewn and placed purposefully where it was. "I find this view to be the best."

She glanced at him over her shoulder. Her bonnet was lying on the ground next to her feet, and a few tendrils of hair had escaped their confines and lifted on the breeze, causing her to tuck them behind her ear. "You may join me if you wish."

He looked at her warily. "Are you certain? Would you not rather find a woodland creature to sit beside you so that I might be forced to find a place on the ground?"

She smiled and chuckled. "No, I do not like sharing my morning respite with wild creatures." Her eyes danced with amusement. She was no doubt attempting to forego adding an impertinent comment.

"But you will make an exception for me?" he teased and then wondered at such a familiar exchange that seemed to fall so easily from his lips.

She laughed, and her laughter was just as delightful as he had imagined it might be, which made him not care in the least why he felt so at ease as to attempt to guess her impertinent response.

"Yes, I will, though I doubt you are ever very wild, Mr. Darcy."

He chuckled as he took a seat next to her. "You would be right. My cousin has attempted to draw me out from my naturally reserved bent, but his efforts have met with very little success." In fact, Miss Elizabeth, in the short time he had known her, had been more successful in drawing him out than his cousin had ever been. That was a thought which was more than a little unsettling. Imagine what would happen if he spent much more time with her?

"Do you only have one cousin just as you only have one sister?" she asked as he removed his hat, placed it on the ground, and made himself as comfortable as he could while feeling rather awkward.

"No." He took in the perspective before him.

"This is a very good observation point. Thank you for sharing it with me."

"It is my pleasure."

He turned his head and arched an eyebrow. "Is it truly your pleasure? I believe you just moments ago told me that returning to London would be an excellent idea."

Her head bobbed up and down slowly as she silently studied the view before them. "I did."

"Why do you think I should return to London?" he pressed.

She turned her face toward him. "How many cousins do you have?"

"Four. Now, tell me why I should return to London." He held her gaze.

"You did not look very happy to be where you were when you said it." Her eyes seemed to challenge him. "Which cousin has attempted to draw you out of yourself?"

"Richard, to me and Georgie — Colonel Fitzwilliam, to most others."

She smiled. "You are close to him then?"

"Very. He is more like a brother to me than a cousin," he said, returning her smile before turning to look out over the landscape again. "We share guardianship of my sister."

"Are you the same age?"

Darcy shook his head. "Richard is two years older than I am." He glanced at her. "Which, before you ask, means he is thirty." His breath caught in his chest. That was likely not the most gentlemanly thing to say.

Her eyes grew wide and her lips parted. "I was not going to ask that!" she cried.

"Were you not?" Surprisingly, his voice sounded much more nonchalant than he felt as he continued down this unfamiliar taunting path. She was tantalizingly expressive and sitting here, conversing with her in such a relaxed and familiar fashion felt so very intimate that a bit of flirting – if that was what he was doing, and he hoped he was – seemed only natural.

"No." She ducked her head slightly and smiled sheepishly. "I was wondering it and wanted to ask, but it would have been impolite. Therefore, I find I must thank you for saving me from the anguish of unsatisfied curiosity."

"It was my pleasure."

They fell into a companionable silence until it was broken by Miss Elizabeth.

"Is he on the continent?"

"My cousin?"

She nodded.

"Thankfully, no."

"I am glad for you." The words were spoken softly as if she was unsure if she should say them.

"Do you have many cousins?" he asked to turn the subject a little but not really knowing what other topic to present. "I know you have an aunt and uncle in town and another aunt and uncle in Hertfordshire, but I know nothing beyond that."

"I have the same number of cousins as you do."

"Are they in town, in Hertfordshire, or both?"

"They are in town."

"All of them?"

She laughed. "Do not sound so surprised, Mr. Darcy. It is not unusual for families to have more than one or two children."

"I apologize. I did not mean to sound surprised."

"And I am only teasing you and not truly offended," she assured him. "And before you ask, they are all younger than me by many years. However, their mother – my aunt Gardiner – is only... well, she is not yet your age."

He blinked. "Indeed?" His head tipped. "I suppose that makes sense as ladies do tend to marry earlier than gentlemen do."

"Yes, most do." There was a trace of amusement in her tone.

"I had not actually considered how old various mothers were," he explained quickly, "which, I am certain, is rather unthinking of me."

"I do not make a habit of thinking about such things either," she assured him. "I will often think one lady is young and one is not, as one might naturally notice, but I rarely consider the age of a mother unless it is already known to me."

"That makes sense." He picked up his hat and began turning it in his hands. "I fear I am at the end of my ability to carry the conversation," he admitted. "I have never excelled at it," he added with a shrug when she looked his direction.

"Truly?"

He nodded. Why had he told her that? He never revealed his flaws to others. He left those for them to discover, and rarely, did he care what others thought about those flaws when they were discovered. However, at present, he felt very much like a young child waiting for his tutor to approve of his work.

"You do not seem the sort to be lost for words."

"I do not?"

"No. Admittedly, we have not had very many opportunities to speak together, but until now, you have never been without something to say."

"Our meetings have been brief."

She allowed that to be true.

Quietly, he drew and released a breath while sending a silent prayer heavenward that his request would not be refused out of hand. He swallowed and then launched into what he had to say before he could think himself out of doing so.

"I would not be opposed to more frequent or longer meetings. I think..." He paused to breathe. A galloping heart seemed to require more frequent breathing. "What I mean to say is that I would like for us to be friends. Is that possible? I know I was rude upon our first meeting or, rather, before our first meeting, but I assure you that I am not always so. I will not say I am never so, because, well, I am, as you have witnessed. But it is not a regular practice –"

He stopped speaking for she had begun laughing softly.

"Did I say something amiss?" He tried to go back through his words.

"No, everything you said was perfect. It is just that for a man who claims to be a gentleman of few words, that was a great number of them and in a very short period of time, Mr. Darcy."

He could feel his ears burning. "I assure you that I do not normally ramble on about things." He shook his head.

"Are you thinking of returning to town again?"

"What? Why do you ask that?" Was she so eager and determined to get rid of him that she was telling him to leave?

"You look very much at present as you did right before you said that earlier." She placed a hand on his forearm. "I apologize. I was teasing, and I have gone too far." She closed her eyes and sighed. "Perhaps *I* should go to London. I despise it when I am teased too far, and yet, here I sit, doing that very thing to another."

He covered her hand with his before she could withdraw her touch. How comforting that small hand on his arm and under his own hand felt. "I am not offended," he assured her. "And, yes, I was thinking of returning to London."

She blinked. "Why?"

He shrugged and shook his head. Why he felt as he did was not something he wished to acknowledge, and yet, his mouth seemed willing to make admissions without his permission.

"I feel a bit turned around." More than a little,

truth be told, but thankfully, his wayward tongue remained silent.

She smiled in response. "New places will do that to some. Is that why you wished to see as much of the land as you could this morning?"

Was it? "Perhaps."

She looked at him expectantly, and he held his tongue between his teeth until she sighed and turned back to looking out across the fields and houses of Hertfordshire.

"May we be friends?"

She glanced his direction. Indecision furrowed her brow. "You know that you were rude?"

"Yes, and I am sorry for it." He had likely never been so sorry for any words he had ever spoken as he was for the ones he had used to protest Bingley's urging him to dance.

She looked at him for a moment longer before a small smile formed on her lips. "Then, yes, I believe we can try to be friends."

Chapter 7

"Father is planning a dinner party for next week." Charlotte linked her arm with Elizabeth's where they stood outside the church the following morning.

"Is that what they are talking about now?" Elizabeth had been watching her father and Simon. The two of them had been very talkative. Nearly everyone who passed them received a greeting. Such a thing was not unusual for Simon, but her father was not usually so animated. Just a few moments ago, Sir William had joined them.

"I believe so," Charlotte answered.

The two of them began strolling in the direction of Longbourn. Not because they were both going there, but because it would move them to a place where a conversation could be had with a greater chance of it not becoming gossip.

"Mr. Newell has been at Longbourn for some time now."

Elizabeth did not miss the implication in her friend's tone. "Unfortunately."

"Will he stay much longer?"

"He leaves tomorrow," she sighed. "However, if he knows about your father's soiree, he will likely return for it."

"If he does not call before then. His home is not so very far away, you know, and the way he has been eyeing Mr. Darcy, I dare say he will return before too many days have passed."

"What do you mean? What does Mr. Darcy have to do with Simon staying at home or returning to call?"

Charlotte laughed. "Mr. Darcy has done a very poor job of keeping his eyes from wandering to you all morning."

Had he, indeed? Elizabeth glanced in Mr. Darcy's direction just in time to see him look away quickly.

"You see what I mean?" Charlotte whispered.

"I still do not see what that has to do with Simon."

"Eliza Bennet, do not play stupid."

"I am not," Elizabeth replied with a flutter of lashes. "I merely do not like what you are implying."

"Ignoring the fact that Mr. Darcy is enamoured with you will not make it less true."

"He is not..." Elizabeth cried before lowering her voice to a whisper, "enamoured with me. We are merely friends. Barely more than acquaintances, truth be told."

"Oh, no, my dear, that gentleman is smitten." She smiled. "With you. And Mr. Newell knows it and is jealous."

Elizabeth could not stand and listen to Charlotte any longer. Both the idea of Mr. Darcy being smitten with her and Simon being jealous made her very uneasy for she did not wish to be the object of either gentleman's affection. Or she was almost completely positive that she did not wish for either gentleman to admire her. She glanced once more at Mr. Darcy. Her unease increased. She needed to move, and so, she began walking further down the road that would take her home.

Charlotte followed.

"You know that Mr. Newell has been hoping for some time that you would pay him particular attention as more than a friend, do you not?"

Elizabeth closed her eyes. "Yes." She wished he would not, for there was no way he was going to ever be anything more than a friend in her mind. Simply put, he was not the sort of gentleman she wished to marry.

"He is handsome," Charlotte said, peeking over her shoulder toward the people they had left behind. "And he is amiable and has a sizable fortune."

"But he is Simon!"

There was more to finding a husband than just knowing that he could carry a conversation with aplomb, had a fine figure, and was comfortably situated financially. Those were admirable traits with which to begin one's search. However, they were not enough to sustain a life-long attachment. At least, they were not for her. She wanted a husband with whom she could have a rousing discussion without it devolving into teasing when the gentleman found he was at the end of his knowledge before she was.

Simon was not stupid. He was a highly intelligent gentleman, but his intelligence was not the sort that could challenge hers as she wished to be challenged. They were equals in most things, but in a few, she was the superior. She hoped that it would not be the same with every gentleman she met.

Perhaps if Simon caused her heart to flutter or made her smile as Jane smiled at the mention of Mr. Bingley, perhaps then, she could more easily accept Simon's love of teasing and his lack of knowledge in some areas more easily.

"He would make a fine husband," Charlotte continued.

"Not for me!" Elizabeth stopped walking and spun toward Charlotte. "Do *you* like him?"

Charlotte's eyes grew wide. "I... I... I have never considered it." Her cheeks flushed brilliantly.

"You *do* like him. You never blush so much as you are now unless you are lying." Elizabeth wanted to do a little jig of delight but refrained. "That is wonderful. Simply wonderful. I could match you with him."

"Lizzy, no," Charlotte protested. "You know where my heart lies."

"With Mr. Reed? Still?"

Charlotte nodded. "Though I am beginning to think I might have to dress in a woolly frock and wander the fields, bleating, before he will pay me any notice."

Elizabeth chuckled. "He is rather devoted to his flock, is he not?"

"It is not a bad thing, for that is why his farm is so profitable, but..."

Elizabeth wrapped her arm tightly around Charlotte's. "Aw, Charlotte. I wish I could make him see what he is missing."

"That makes two of us."

"Have you considered Mr. Newell?" She was certain that Charlotte's response to her question about liking that gentleman had been a lie.

"I have, but my heart would not be swayed."

"Do you think you could try again?"

"Elizabeth!"

Elizabeth sighed. "I just wish he would find someone to replace me."

Charlotte chuckled. "And then who will you marry? Mr. Darcy?"

"No," Elizabeth snapped. "I have not yet found my true love, and there is no rush to do so."

"I would not wait too long," Charlotte said softly. "The future comes more quickly than one would think."

Again, Elizabeth hugged her friend's arm close. She knew that Charlotte was beginning to despair that she would ever marry, and it hurt Elizabeth's heart to see her friend so despondent.

Charlotte was a wonderful lady. She was patient and kind, and she knew all that there could possibly be to know about keeping a family well-fed and in good health. Her mother had taught her well, and her two younger brothers, as well as her younger sister, had put that knowledge to the test many times. Any gentleman, who chose to marry Charlotte, would find himself safely ensconced in an exceptionally organized and peaceful home with Charlotte at its helm.

"Acceptable gentlemen are not in plentiful supply in Meryton, nor will they be for some time with all that is happening in the world." Charlotte shook her head. "We have lost so many from our numbers already to the colonies and the continent. Please, Lizzy, please, promise me that you will consider Mr. Darcy since you will not consider Mr. Newell."

"Oh, Charlotte."

"Please, Lizzy."

Elizabeth hated to deny her friend this wish, but she truly did not want to consider Mr. Darcy, though, she had to admit that, since his apology yesterday, it was harder to find a suitable reason to continue in her dislike for him.

"I will promise you that I will consider Mr. Darcy, if, and only if, you will promise me that you will consider Mr. Newell as an alternative to Mr. Reed."

"But I have considered him," Charlotte protested.

"It is the only way I will promise to do what you have asked."

Charlotte scowled and blew out a frustrated breath.

Good, she was feeling exactly as Elizabeth was – irritated and displeased.

"Very well," Charlotte finally agreed. "I will consider Mr. Newell if you will consider Mr. Darcy."

"Truly? You are going to agree to it?" Elizabeth had been confident that Charlotte would not make such a promise.

"Yes. This way, at least one of us, if not both, will find herself happily married."

"Happily?"

Charlotte laughed. "Perhaps."

They stepped further to the side of the road as a carriage drew near.

"Ladies," Mr. Bingley called from the window, "are you both going to Longbourn?"

"No," Charlotte replied. "I am taking the next left to Lucas Lodge."

Mr. Bingley poked his head out the window

and looked ahead of them. "That is not very far, is it?"

"No, not at all," Charlotte assured him.

"And then, are you walking the rest of the way to Longbourn alone, Miss Elizabeth?"

"I had planned to." She turned her head toward Charlotte who had poked her in the side with her elbow. Oh, dear, Mr. Newell was walking very rapidly in their direction.

"Would you rather ride with your sisters?" Mr. Bingley was looking in the same direction that Elizabeth had been. "Unless you are hoping for Mr. Newell to accompany you."

"No," the word flew from Elizabeth's mouth. She had no desire to walk alone for a mile with Mr. Newell. "I would welcome the comfort and speed of a carriage."

Mr. Bingley grinned broadly. "Then, please, allow me to help you aboard."

"But Charlotte..."

"She can ride with us to the turn." He had climbed down and was already offering his hand to Charlotte who took it and got into the carriage. Then, he turned to Elizabeth.

"Thank you," Elizabeth said as she placed her hand in his and stepped up into the vehicle where she froze, not knowing what to do. Jane, Mary, and Charlotte filled one bench, and across from them sat Mr. Darcy and two empty places.

"You may sit beside me," Mr. Darcy offered.

"Thank you," she muttered as she took a seat on his left, leaving the seat next to the window, from which Mr. Bingley had addressed her, open for Mr. Bingley.

"Your mother has graciously invited us to dine with you this afternoon," Darcy explained.

"Has she?" Elizabeth looked to Jane for confirmation.

"She has," Mary answered.

"Just you." She pointed to her bench mates.

"Oh, no," Mary answered again. "The Lucases and Mr. Newell have also been invited, although I suppose Mr. Newell was understood to have been included since he will be with us until tomorrow morning."

"And Mr. Bingley's sisters and Mr. Hurst?"

"They declined –"

"Thankfully," Mr. Bingley muttered, causing Mary to smile as she continued her explanation.

"Netherfield's cook would be expecting someone to eat what she has prepared and so, they thought they should return to Netherfield. It was all very spontaneous," Mary explained.

"I see." Elizabeth leaned back for a moment and then popped forward. "All the Lucases were invited?" She looked at Charlotte who shrugged.

"Yes, but Sir William has left it to each of his children to decide for themselves. Therefore, Maria will be joining our younger sisters."

"And the boys?" Charlotte asked Mary since Mary was the one who seemed eager to give details regarding the party.

Mary smiled. "Mother refuses to allow any dancing."

"So they are going home?"

"Yes. Sitting in a drawing room and reading or conversing did not interest them, especially since they will not have a chance to flirt with Lydia and Kitty so easily," Mary added.

"If you knew all this, why did Mr. Bingley

offer to only take Charlotte to the turn to Lucas Lodge?"

Mr. Bingley smiled and settled further into his seat. "I knew that the explanation would take some time and thought it most expedient to be on our way before Mr. Newell reached you. Therefore, I fibbed." He sat forward. "Was I wrong to assume you preferred to ride with us rather than walk with Mr. Newell?"

"No, you were not wrong."

"I am glad to hear it." Bingley settled back in his seat once again.

"As am I," Darcy agreed softly, though Elizabeth chose to ignore it, and the carriage fell into silence until Jane commented on the orchard, drawing Mr. Bingley and, in turn, Mr. Darcy into a conversation about growing fruit and the benefits of such an effort.

Thankfully, no one called on Elizabeth to add her thoughts on the matter because she was far too busy thinking about Mr. Darcy's whispered agreement with his friend and about how sitting next to him was not nearly so uncomfortable as she had imagined it would be when she first entered the carriage.

Soon enough, they were home and, as Elizabeth passed the dining room, she noticed that it was laid out for a large crowd. Surely, there was no way for Mama to have gotten word to Mrs. Hill about the unexpected guests, for Mama and Papa had not yet arrived.

"I thought this was a spontaneous dinner party?" she whispered to Mary while Jane made certain that Mr. Bingley and Mr. Darcy would be comfortable in the sitting room alone while she and her sisters went upstairs to remove their bonnets and such.

"It was spontaneous only in that our guests did not receive an invitation until moments before they left the church."

"Then it was planned?"

Mary nodded.

"Why?"

"Because, my dear sister, while Mr. Newell might have a sizable income and a fine estate and while he might have mentioned his desire to speak with you privately –"

Elizabeth gasped, and Mary nodded knowingly before continuing.

"Mr. Darcy has ten thousand and, according to Mama, favours you. Therefore, there was no need to limit your choice to just Mr. Newell, as lovely as he is." She blew out a breath. "Apparently, Simon might do very well for me."

Elizabeth caught a laugh before it could be more than a small outburst. "Do you wish it?"

Mary shook her head. "Not particularly. I know he is handsome, but I am not –"

"Do not say that!" Elizabeth cried before Mary could continue her explanation. "You are handsome. We were just *blessed* with a sister who shines above all others and with whom we must be compared."

Mary chuckled at that. "I am not even as pretty as you, but that is not the point. I do not find myself drawn to Simon."

Elizabeth understood that. She glanced over her shoulder. "Then, might I suggest you direct him towards Charlotte?"

Chapter 8

Mrs. Bennet bustled into the drawing room no more than twenty minutes after she had entered the house. "We will have a cup of tea and a light lunch now and our meal later." She smoothed the cloth that a maid had just laid on a small table near the door. "As my husband said at the church, it will be nothing formal today. We are just gathering to enjoy one another's company." She smiled and took a seat. "The tea will be here soon." She paused. "It is a delightfully fine day, is it not, Mr. Darcy?"

"Indeed, it is, Madame."

"If I remember correctly, you like to walk, do you not?"

"Yes, I do."

"Excellent. And, Mr. Bingley, you also favour the activity, do you not?"

"I do," Bingley assured her.

"It would not do to be traipsing hither and yon across the wilderness, but a stroll in the garden might be just the thing. Both Jane and Elizabeth like to walk. They can accompany you."

Miss Elizabeth's cheeks grew rosy while Miss Bennet seemed unaffected by the comment except for a tightening of her smile. From his seat near the window, Mr. Newell coughed softly, causing Mrs. Bennet to look in his direction.

"I had hoped to –" he began but Mrs. Bennet did not allow him to finish his sentence.

"I did not mean only Mr. Darcy, Mr. Bingley, Elizabeth, and Jane could go into the garden," Mrs. Bennet assured him. "I just did not wish for our guests to feel unattended, for I dare say I will not be able to accompany you. There are things to prepare, you see."

"Yes, but –" Mr. Newell began again.

"Elizabeth, would you please get my shawl? It is a fine day, but I am feeling a bit cool."

Mr. Newell moved forward as if he was going to follow Elizabeth, but Mrs. Bennet once again inserted herself between the gentleman and his plans.

"Mary, please go with Elizabeth."

Miss Mary's brow furrowed, but she said nothing as she rose to go with her sister. It seemed to Darcy that there was some reason why Mrs. Bennet was keeping Mr. Newell from her daughter. He turned his eyes toward the gentleman, who was currently resembling a small storm cloud. Frustration would soon be oozing from him if Mrs. Bennet continued as she had been.

"Tables," the woman declared. "We should see that the card tables are brought out."

"If you direct me, I can assist with that," Bingley offered.

"I can as well," Darcy said.

"As can I." Mr. Newell shot Darcy a disparaging look.

That seemed odd.

It did not take long to arrange the room according to Mrs. Bennet's plans, and Darcy was just retaking his seat, when the Lucases, as well as Miss Elizabeth and Miss Mary, entered the room. Mr. Bennet and the tea service and a tray of rolls, cheese, and biscuits followed closely on their heels, and the room began to feel rather full. However, even with a large group gathered and the noise and commotion that such a crowd might bring to such a situation, the distribution of tea and food progressed smoothly.

It was impressive, to Darcy, how Mrs. Bennet took control of the room and with a nod or a look, had each of her daughters doing their part to assist. It was not at all what he had expected from a lady who had, to this point, only appeared flighty and scattered. It seemed Mrs. Bennet was a consummate hostess despite her exuberance, and her daughters had benefited from her instruction.

Miss Elizabeth would be an excellent choice as the mistress of an estate, perhaps even Pemberley. Darcy coughed and sputtered as he attempted to expel the tea he had inhaled instead of swallowing. He had never had such a thought about any particular young lady before – except for Caroline. However, when thinking of Caroline as a possible mistress of Pemberley, it had been done over a glass of port and with the same diligence one might use when considering whom to hire as a housekeeper or cook. It had not been a sudden inspiration sort of thing as his thought just now had been. There had been little pleasure in the prospect of marrying Caroline if he were to be honest with himself.

"I am well," he finally managed to say to his hostess who was all concern. He patted the front of his waistcoat where he had spilled a bit of tea when the coughing fit had begun. "I swallowed wrong," he explained.

"It seems, Mr. Darcy," Miss Lucas, who was seated next to him, said with a smile, "that you are not to be trusted with cups of liquid when in company with Bennet ladies."

He chuckled. "Indeed," he replied. "I am not usually so clumsy."

"No, I would not take you for a gentleman who stumbles and bumbles his way through life," she assured him.

"I thank you for the compliment." He glanced at Miss Elizabeth who was sitting next to her friend. "However, I may have misspoken."

"Is that so?" Miss Lucas's eyebrows rose in interest.

"I fear that I do, on occasion, stumble and bumble." He drew a silent fortifying breath. A little embarrassment was a small price to pay to prove himself a gentleman, was it not? "In my speech."

Her brow furrowed. "How so?"

He glanced at Elizabeth again. "I fear I said something untrue and very ungentlemanly at the assembly. I am certain you know of what I speak."

Her replying smile was confirmation that she did indeed know to what he referred.

"It is a dreadful fault, and one I own." He took a careful sip from his cup. "I have, of course, made my apology to the individual whom my words injured."

Miss Lucas's lips twitched as if she were attempting to contain her amusement. "I do hope you were forgiven."

"Not readily, but I think I have been."

"Some people just have a difficult time amending their opinions, do they not?" She cast a look of some significance at Elizbeth, who scowled briefly.

Darcy finished the tea in his cup and no sooner had he lowered it to his saucer than Mrs. Bennet was suggesting they all walk in the garden. It was almost as if she had been waiting for him to finish.

Bingley was, as was his normal enthusiastic way, the first to rise from his place and offer his hand to Miss Bennet.

While Miss Bennet accepted his friend's offer, Darcy prepared to make a similar offer to Miss Elizabeth. Unfortunately, he was not quick enough.

"Miss Elizabeth, may I escort you?" Mr. Newell asked before Miss Bennet had finished agreeing to walk with Bingley.

"I believe that my mother wished for me to accompany Mr. Darcy."

"Miss Lucas or Miss Mary can do that," Mr. Newell countered.

"I am certain they are capable of doing as you suggest, Mr. Newell –"

"Simon," he corrected.

Elizabeth ignored him and continued, "How-ever, neither they nor you will have to bear my mother's displeasure. That will be for me alone."

Mr. Newell took her hand and placed it on his arm with a smile. "I will tell her that I insisted."

Elizabeth pulled her hand away from Mr. Newell. "And what if I do not wish to walk with you?"

That seemed to take Mr. Newell by surprise as he pulled back as if he had been struck. "I apolo-gize. You are right. I was being too forward. With whom would you like to walk?" It sounded as if it took a considerable amount of effort for the words to be said pleasantly. "Me or Mr. Darcy?"

"Truthfully?"

Mr. Newell nodded as the muscles in his jaw flexed.

"In all honesty, I would like to walk with Charlotte," Elizabeth replied with a smile. "However, that is not what my mother wishes, and as I have already mentioned, I do not relish the thought of a lecture. Therefore, I must choose Mr. Darcy, but I would be most grateful if you would take my place in walking with Charlotte."

"How grateful?" Mr. Newell asked with a frown. "Grateful enough that you might allow me the privilege of a private conversation later?"

Ah! Was that what Mrs. Bennet had been attempting to prevent? Did she not wish for her daughter to entertain an offer from Mr. Newell? From what Darcy knew of the man – which was all that Caroline had expounded on to him at length after his first meeting Mr. Newell at Longbourn — Mr. Newell was not an undesirable match. He was not as wealthy or well-connected as Darcy was...

Oh, things were beginning to make sense. Mrs. Bennet preferred him as a suitor for her daughter instead of Mr. Newell. Oddly, the thought did not disturb Darcy as he thought it might. Normally, he removed himself from any situation which bore a hint of matchmaking, but at present, the idea of being pushed toward Elizabeth was not unpleasant. In fact, it was enough to make him smile despite the knowledge that Elizabeth was only agreeing to accompany him in the garden because she wished to avoid a lecture.

"Well, then, Miss Elizabeth." Mr. Darcy extended his arm to her, earning another scowl from Mr. Newell. However, this time, Darcy neither found it strange nor did he wonder about its source. The man was jealous, and while that should make Darcy feel somewhat sorry for the man, it did not. He frowned. What was becoming of him?

Elizabeth placed her hand on his arm.

"And what about our meeting later?"

Newell was persistent. Not that Darcy would blame him. Elizabeth was worth a bit of a fight. He shook his head. Returning to town before he found himself as irrevocably smitten with the lovely Miss Elizabeth Bennet as Newell seemed to be was likely a good plan. He had proved himself to be a gentleman. He had done what he had determined to do. There was no need to pursue his plan further. And yet, the thought of not continuing his demonstration of gentlemanliness made him feel as if he was only giving half a report to his tutor.

"That I cannot promise," Elizabeth said to Newell, "for I do not know my mother's plans for this party, and I must remain available to assist her."

Newell had by this point offered his arm, reluctantly, to Miss Lucas and was following behind Darcy. "Surely, you could spare five minutes. I will speak to your father, and he will arrange it."

Elizabeth remained silent until they had gotten so far as the border to the garden. Then, she removed her hand and from Darcy's arm and turned to Newell. "I believe you have already spoken to my father, and there is no need for us to speak privately. Do not push me, Simon."

"What do you mean there is no need?"

Darcy caught Miss Lucas's eye and nodded toward the path. It was best if he and she were to be a distance away to give Newell a bit of privacy since it did not seem that his suit was going to be met with any sort of success.

"We are friends, Simon, and I would like to keep it that way."

"But we could be more..."

"I would have waited," Darcy whispered to Miss Lucas.

"He could wait for three years, and it would not help him," she replied just as softly.

"Is that so?" Darcy glanced back at Elizabeth. "From what I hear from Miss Bingley, Mr. Newell is a worthy prospect."

"He is," Miss Lucas agreed. "However, he has not touched Miss Elizabeth's heart, and she is not so old that she must find a situation regardless of her heart's desires." She sighed. "And she is far too stubborn to think that she might have to accept such an outcome."

Darcy's brow furrowed. "Do you mean she would rather be a spinster than marry without love?"

"That is exactly what I mean, Mr. Darcy."

They had stopped a distance from where Elizabeth and Newell were still talking, though it looked as if they had nearly completed their conversation.

"Whoever wishes to claim Elizabeth as his wife will have to lay claim to her heart." Miss Lucas looked at him and held his gaze.

Was she suggesting... No. Surely, she was not, was she? He looked from her to Elizabeth who as now walking towards them while Mr. Newell was heading back to the house. When he returned his eyes to Miss Lucas, her left eyebrow arched, and her expression challenged him to deny that he had not already considered Elizabeth as a possible choice for his wife.

He gave her a sharp nod of his head. There was no use denying it. She seemed to be far too sensible a lady to believe him if he did try to deny the truth. "Thank you. I will keep that in mind."

He was rewarded with a knowing smile. Then, she turned toward her friend. "Have you chased away my escort, Eliza?"

Elizabeth shook her head. "It was not my doing. I tried to avoid it."

"I have two arms," Darcy offered.

"Thank you," she smiled softly at him and placed her hand on his arm.

"Is he well?" Darcy asked as they began walking.

"I do not know. I hope so." She sighed. It was a sound filled with worry.

"Are you well?"

"I will be. I have never refused a gentleman before."

Darcy chuckled. "Have you not? I seem to remember you refusing to dance with someone not so very long ago."

"That is not the same!"

Miss Lucas laughed aloud.

"It is not!" Elizabeth repeated with a glare for her friend.

"Rejection is rejection, and while many a gentleman would not wish to admit to this, our hearts are not made of stone. Some of us bruise easily. I had the advantage of not having my heart engaged, so the damage was only to my pride."

They walked on for a few paces in silence.

"Do you think his heart was engaged?" Elizabeth asked.

"Did Mr. Newell not declare his love for you?" Darcy asked.

"No. He merely said we would suit for we are such good friends. Of course, I did not give him time to make a proper offer."

"Simon has paid particular attention to you," Miss Lucas offered.

Had he? That was interesting.

"I know," Elizabeth whispered.

"Perhaps his disappointment will not be too long in duration," Darcy offered.

"I pray you are correct. I also hope that neither my mother's nor my father's disappointment will be too great."

"I cannot speak for your father, but I dare say your mother will be delighted with your refusal," Darcy offered. "She seemed intent upon keeping you separated from Mr. Newell earlier."

Elizabeth groaned. "You noticed that?"

He nodded. "Whatever her plans are for you," he said as if he did not have a good idea of what they were, "I doubt you will be reprimanded too severely for your refusal just now."

"Just do not disappoint her again," Miss Lucas added, earning herself a glare.

So, Mr. Newell was not Elizabeth's choice, but neither was he. That was a good thing though, was it not? He was not seeking to be matched with Elizabeth, was he? He had considered her and had even admitted as much to her friend. But he did not truly wish to be matched with her, did he? Oh, his mind was in such a muddled mess! Perhaps a trip to town would do him some good.

Chapter 9

Using a hand to shade her eyes from the late morning sun, Elizabeth attempted to make out who the rider was in the field to the left of the road.

Mary placed the basket she was carrying on the ground and joined Elizabeth near the hedgerow which bordered the road. "It looks like Mr. Darcy."

It did indeed look like Mr. Darcy. He was an excellent rider and being seated on a horse did not detract from his fine figure. Elizabeth was glad for the coolness of the day so that the blush such a thought brought to her cheeks might be thought of as a result of being from the cold.

"Who is with him?" Mary asked as a second rider joined Mr. Darcy. "It does not look like Mr. Bingley for Mr. Bingley is not so broad as that."

"I have no idea. He does not look familiar at all." Elizabeth tipped her head and studied the pair of men.

The stranger called something to Mr. Darcy and then both set off racing down the field.

"He must be a friend of Mr. Darcy," Elizabeth commented.

If only they would come in her direction so that her curiosity could be assuaged. But, alas, they were riding away from her rather than toward her.

"We should get this food delivered." Elizabeth picked up the basket Mary had put down, and the pair resumed walking toward their destination, a tenant's cottage only a half-mile from where they were standing.

Mrs. Thompson's baby had arrived two days ago on Sunday evening. Mama had visited yesterday and promised a basket of soup and bread, which is what Elizabeth was now carrying.

"Miss Elizabeth! Miss Mary!" A little lad, wearing a skeleton suit, ran out to meet them as they entered the walk in front of the house. He clung to a cat that was vociferously decrying its predicament.

"Is this Miss Scratches?" Mary asked as she crouched down to greet the boy, who giggled and allowed Mary to take the cat.

"See." He held an arm out to show her a fresh scratch. The cat had been given the name Miss Scratches because of the number of times she had scratched little John Thompson when he attempted to play with her.

"You must stop picking Miss Scratches up," Mary reprimanded softly. "It appears she does not like it, and scrapes and scratches can be very painful if not tended properly."

Mary released the cat she held and took the boy's hand. "Come. We will see what can be done for your scratch, and then you can tell me all about your baby sister."

"She cries a lot," the boy said as he walked with Mary.

"Many babies do," Mary assured him.

Mary was a natural with children. She could scold and direct in such a fashion that the child never seemed to be completely out of sorts with her. If only she could master the same skill with their younger sisters, for Lydia and Kitty never accepted scolding from Mary without a protest or sulking.

"Thank you, miss," the Thompson's maid of all work said as she took the basket from Elizabeth.

"Do you have some salve for a scratch?" Mary asked.

"Yes, miss." The maid gave the little boy a stern look. "John, what did your mama say about the cat?"

The youngster hung his head. "Not to pester her."

"If you will follow me to the kitchen," she said to Mary. "The missus is in her room sitting by the window. It was such a sunny day that we thought it would do her more good to see the light than lie in bed with the drapes drawn."

Elizabeth followed them down the corridor, but only to the room behind the staircase. "Mrs. Thompson," she said as she slowly opened the door.

"Come in. Come in."

"Mary is with me," Elizabeth said as she entered the room and sat down on the bench at the foot of the bed. "She is seeing to a scratch."

"Was my son carrying the cat again?"

Elizabeth nodded.

"I should think that, with as many scratches as it gives him, he would learn to leave it be." Mrs. Thompson shook her head.

"Determination is a good trait," Elizabeth smiled at Mrs. Thompson when her brows rose quickly. "Eventually, it will be a good thing, though I know that it is a trial at present. I imagine he will not be one to blindly follow others."

Mrs. Thompson sighed. "I worry about the children who will follow him. I pray he does not lead them down a wrong path."

"I very much doubt he will. John has loving parents, who are just as determined to see him grow into a fine young man as he is in making Miss Scratches enjoy being held."

Mrs. Thompson laughed. "I hope that Julia is an easy child."

"My mother hoped that four times," Elizabeth

said with a laugh. "None of us younger girls were as easy as Jane."

"Ah, but you are such lovely young ladies." Her head tipped. "Or will be. I think your youngest sisters are still growing into their loveliness. They are spirited."

"Very," Elizabeth agreed. "However, I have noticed a bit of a tempering in Kitty, so there is hope."

"That is precisely what your mother said!"

"Is it, indeed?" How curious. Elizabeth did not think that her mother was disturbed by the liveliness of her youngest daughters, but perhaps she was.

"Welcome, Miss Mary," Mrs. Thompson said as Mary slipped into the room and went directly to the cradle to see the new arrival.

"John made me promise to see his sister first before I did anything else," she explained.

Elizabeth joined her sister. "She is adorable."

"She has curly brown hair just like her brother and the same nose." Mrs. Thompson gently touched the cheek of her sleeping child. "But her eyes. Ah, they look just like her father's. John's are more like mine."

"You are blessed to have such a precious gift," Mary said before taking her seat next to Elizabeth on the bench. "We do not wish to tire you, so you must tell us to go if we stay too long."

"I am tired all day long," she replied. "It is how it is for a mother. You do what you must for your children with little thought for yourself – or, at least, with little time to think about yourself," she said with a laugh. "It grows easier as they get older and begin sleeping better." She paused and stroked her daughter's cheek again. "But you worry. You always worry." She smiled. "For now, I worry about them being strong and healthy, and later, I will worry about them starting their own family."

While she watched Mrs. Thompson lift her now awake baby from the cradle, Elizabeth thought about her conversation with Mr. Darcy about the ages of mothers. Mrs. Thompson was likely not more than five years older than Elizabeth, but she seemed so much wiser. Elizabeth wondered if that wisdom just came to a lady when she began running her own home and had her first child, or if it was something one must possess before marrying. Jane was wise like Mrs. Thompson, and Mary was all that was practical at times – had she not just demonstrated a few moments ago when dealing with John's scratch that she was capable of being a wonderful mother. Elizabeth, however, was not certain she possessed enough practicality or wisdom to be a mother.

"You look rather pensive, Miss Elizabeth," Mrs. Thompson said.

Elizabeth blushed at being caught woolgathering.

"I apologize." She paused, considered if she should share what she was thinking, and then, before she could think too far and prevent herself from speaking, she said, "I was just pondering what it must be like to be a mother. It seems a daunting task."

"That it is," Mrs. Thompson said. "And, truth be told, none of us are truly prepared for the position until it is thrust upon us, screeching and squawking and searching for food. You will do well."

"Thank you." Elizabeth hoped Mrs. Thompson was right.

"Will it be soon?" Mrs. Thompson looked up from her nursing infant and smiled at Elizabeth. "I heard there was a handsome and wealthy gentleman who was asking about you at the assembly."

"You did?"

Mrs. Thompson nodded. "Helen had it from Maggie, who had been questioned about you after Miss Lydia spilled a cup of punch."

"Oh." Maggie must have been the maid Charlotte had seen cleaning the floor.

"He seemed quite curious to know what sort of young lady you were and seemed pleased to hear you were as he had thought of you upon meeting."

"Did he?" Charlotte had said as much, had she not?

Mrs. Thompson smiled. "I also hear he danced with you and no one else who was not of his party."

Elizabeth's cheeks felt as if they were on fire, and she was certain they were a deep shade of red.

"I have also heard that he spent more time attending to you than he did the sermon on Sunday."

Oh, my! Charlotte must not have been teasing or exaggerating about that.

"That is all true," Mary said.

"Is it?" Elizabeth turned to look at her sister.

"He did dance with you, and I did see him watching you at church."

"Oh." She drew a quick breath. "Do you think..." She could not bring herself to ask it.

Mary nodded. "Yes, I do think Mr. Darcy admires you if he is not already half in love with you."

Mrs. Thompson laughed. "I do not think I have ever seen a lady look so horrified at being admired by a rich and handsome gentleman."

"No, I am not horrified at the thought of that." She shook her head. "Or I do not think I am."

Her brow furrowed.

"I knew he wished that we could be friends

after he apologized for his insult, but I did not think it was more than that." Or, more precisely, she had not wished for it to be more than that, for the idea had caused the most unsettling feeling. Therefore, she had pushed it away and determined to be civil and amiable but no more than that.

What was she supposed to do now? She could easily persuade herself that Charlotte was wrong, but to convince herself that Charlotte, Mary, Mrs. Thompson, and whoever had told all of these things to Mrs. Thompson were all wrong? Well, that was a bit harder to do.

"My husband said that Mr. Darcy seemed a very fine sort of gentleman – a trifle reserved but not meanly arrogant – and according to Helen, Maggie said the same. Even though she had heard he was rather aloof at the assembly, she did not see any of that when she spoke with him. He was right gentlemanly."

"Oh." It was all that Elizabeth could articulate. Her mind was whirling with thoughts and feelings.

"Are you well?" Mary whispered.

"Yes, yes. I am just surprised." And more than a little overwhelmed by how wrong it appeared she had willfully been.

Again, Mrs. Thompson laughed. "I do hope it is a good surprise."

"I really cannot say," Elizabeth admitted honestly.

Mrs. Thompson lifted her daughter to her shoulder. "In my way of thinking, if this Mr. Darcy is fortunate enough to win your admiration and steal you away from Longbourn, he will have found himself a prize to be envied."

"I doubt that," Elizabeth cried.

"You are too modest," Mrs. Thompson insisted. "Your mother and father have done well by you. The gentleman who owned the land my father tended was not so kind and compassionate as your father. His wife attempted to make up for his shortcomings, but she could only do so much. I know of what I speak, Miss Elizabeth. Your family is a blessing to us."

"Then, I thank you on my family's behalf." As much as she wanted to protest such a statement, she would not offend Mrs. Thompson by telling her that her opinions were unfounded. What did Elizabeth know of unkind landlords?

After a few more minutes of conversing about the new addition to the Thompson family, and, after John had come to see that his guests had properly admired his sister even if she did cry a lot, Mary and Elizabeth took their leave of Mrs. Thompson and began their walk back to Longbourn – Mary with an empty basket in her hand and Elizabeth with a mind filled with a great deal about which to think.

Chapter 10

"Mrs. Bennet was asking about you again today," Bingley said as he slipped into a chair in the library at Netherfield. "Apparently, missing one day of calling to go shooting is understandable, but missing two is not." He chuckled.

"Did you tell her that my cousin has come to visit?" Darcy glanced up quickly from the book he was reading.

Bingley nodded. "She was shocked that you have not introduced him to her, but do not worry, Miss Mary took up your cause and told her mother that would be very unusual. And then, Mrs. Bennet excused herself to locate her husband. I should think we will be getting a call from the gentleman before long."

"And how much about who I am did you tell

Mrs. Bennet?" Colonel Richard Fitzwilliam asked.

"Only as much as she asked," Bingley replied with a smirk.

"In other words," Darcy said dryly, "she knows everything any mother of unwed daughters wishes to know."

Bingley shook his head. "Likely more than that."

"Exactly what did you tell her?" Richard demanded.

"I only shared with her the standard items of importance– you are the second son of an earl, colonel in the regulars, not on the continent at present but had been, have a smallish inheritance, hazel eyes, sandy hair, and approximately my height but broader, thirty-one years of age, unwed, no appearance of being wed any time soon, looking for an heiress, and more of a brother to Darcy than a cousin along with being co-guardian of Darcy's sister."

"Is that all?" Richard shook his head and frowned.

Bingley's brow furrowed as he thought. "No,

no," he finally said. "That is not all. She also knows that you enjoy music, dancing, and reading." He settled into his chair but then popped forward. "And that you do not expect to be in the area for long."

"Did you also tell her that I am not looking for a wife?"

"Of course, but, according to Mrs. Bennet, no gentleman knows he is looking for a wife until he has found one."

Darcy chuckled. "That sounds a great deal like your mother, Richard."

"Indeed, it does. Female logic, if it may be called that, is somewhat lacking in understanding the view of a man's desire to marry."

"How so?" Bingley asked.

"A gentleman knows when he is ready to marry, and then, he sets about finding a wife. It is not as if we are surprised by the notion."

"I was not looking for a wife when I took Netherfield, but I believe I have found one," Bingley countered.

"You have been looking for a wife since you began noticing girls were pretty," Darcy said.

"Not so," Bingley corrected. "I have been looking for what I wish for in a wife. I have not been looking for a wife. The two are very different. It would be very odd if I had been looking for a wife while still a child, do you not think? For I cannot remember a time when I did not notice that girls are pretty."

"This is why Mrs. Bennet could extract so much information from him," Richard said to Darcy with a flourish of his hand in Bingley's direction. "His ways of thinking are as muddled as any –"

"Do not say lady," Bingley growled, causing Richard to chuckle.

"Very well. I shall not say it, but I will think it."

"I have a mind to send a note to Mrs. Bennet and her five daughters, inviting them to dine with us tomorrow."

"Do you hear him, Darcy? He thinks I could be swayed to consider a lady of little means."

"He thinks nothing of the sort." Darcy sighed and closed his book.

There was no hope of being able to concentrate when Bingley and Richard were arguing. One was just as stubborn as the other, and they were also both equally matched in making sport of his opponent.

"He just thinks it would be amusing to see you surrounded by a mother and the daughters she wishes to see married off – which, by the way, would be four and not five." He was thinking of Miss Bennet's marked preference for Bingley, but the thought of Miss Elizabeth flirting with his cousin, which came to mind, caused Darcy a moment of disquiet.

"Three," Bingley countered.

Darcy turned his attention to Bingley. "She has, I believe, claimed you for Miss Bennet. That is only one daughter. That leaves four for her to match with Richard."

Again, a sense of disquiet settled on Darcy as he arched an eyebrow and glared at Bingley hoping that Bingley would leave things at that. So far, Darcy had managed to avoid the topic of Miss Elizabeth since Richard arrived. Not that she had been far from his mind. She never was.

"I do believe Mrs. Bennet has her eye on you for one of her other daughters."

Blast him!

"Why else would she be so concerned that you have not called?" Bingley continued.

"Have you been calling on Bingley's neighbours?" Richard asked.

"I have. It seemed the polite thing to do to help Bingley settle into the neighbourhood."

Bingley laughed. "You did not care about that at all when you were at the assembly." He turned to Richard. "You should have seen how he looked down his nose at my neighbours."

"I was not looking down on them – well, not entirely," Darcy argued. "I was observing them."

"Much as he always does." Bingley gave Richard a speaking look.

"Like this?" Richard lifted his chin and looked coolly around the room.

"Very like that! Now, look at one of my neighbours and then tell me – in her hearing – that she is not handsome enough to tempt you, and you will have him spot on."

Richard's eyes grew wide. "He did not."

"I assure you he did."

"I did not know she heard me," Darcy protested. It was a weak excuse, but it was also the only one that came to mind.

"Oh, but," Bingley leaned toward Richard, his eagerness to share what he knew written clearly on his face, "she made certain Darcy knew she had heard him."

If Bingley's chuckle was any indication, he was thoroughly enjoying sharing his story.

"He asked her to dance, but, from what I heard from my sisters, her refusal of him left him with no doubt that she had heard his comment and that her opinion of his behaviour was not one of approval."

Richard looked at Darcy and then back at Bingley. "Are you still speaking of the neighbour lady who was not tempting enough?"

Bingley nodded.

"Darcy asked her to dance?"

Again, Bingley nodded while looking excessively amused.

"I apologized," Darcy inserted. "Now, could we, please, move on to other things?"

"This lady. The one who was not tempting enough and refused Darcy. Is she one of Mrs. Bennet's daughters?"

Why was it always so hard to move his cousin off a topic that piqued his curiosity?

"There is a reason you are a colonel," Bingley said with a smile. "He is quite intelligent, is he not, Darcy?"

"Indubitably," Darcy said flatly. "When are you returning to town, Richard?" Hopefully, that would keep them from discussing Miss Elizabeth any further.

"No earlier than I have already told you – a week from today."

"I was thinking I might return with you. I would like to see how Georgiana is doing." He stood and placed his book on the table before walking to the window. "I would not be gone for too long," he said with a glance toward Bingley. "Just long enough to assure myself that my sister is well. I know my promise to you, and I will not neglect it."

However, he needed to be away from Hertfordshire – and Miss Elizabeth – for he had done nothing but think of her for days now. He needed some time and space to clear his mind and get over this fascination with Miss Elizabeth Bennet – if such a thing could even be done.

"Georgiana is making excellent progress in her studies," Richard said. "My mother is very pleased with the effect of Mrs. Annesley's company."

"I would still like to see it with my own eyes."

He had left his sister's future to another before, trusting that all was being done and reported as it should be. He would not be duped a second time. Not that he expected his aunt to dupe him, but he did not want to discover that his aunt had been played for a fool by a practised liar as both he and his sister had been.

"A week Thursday, you say?" Bingley asked.

"Yes, a week Thursday," Richard replied.

"I shall secure an invitation for you to Sir William's dinner party. It is on Wednesday. He can then add having had an earl's son dine with him to his list of accomplishments. He has been to St. James Palace, you see."

"And he is quite proud of that fact," Darcy added without turning from the window.

"He is not a bad sort of person, though," Bingley added quickly. "I would not have you thinking ill of him before you even meet him, but I would have you prepared."

"He has endured worse," Darcy assured Bingley. "You have met our aunt, Lady Catherine, have you not?"

Bingley laughed but did not get to say anything in response as Mr. Bennet was announced and introductions were made.

"My wife," Mr. Bennet said apologetically to Bingley, "was insistent that I greet your guest on her behalf." He sighed and turned to Darcy. "And she wished for me to share with you her desire to see you again."

"I will call soon." It seemed the best thing to say, even if the thought of the pleasure of seeing Miss Elizabeth warred with the urge to flee to London.

"Newell has a bit more business with Phillips and will be arriving on Sunday," Mr. Bennet continued, "but that does not mean you cannot call as well."

"That is very generous of you," Darcy said.

"Generosity has nothing to do with it. Lizzy does not wish to marry the man, but he seems unwilling to give up his suit." Mr. Bennet shook his head. "I cannot blame him."

Neither could Darcy. Miss Elizabeth would be a challenge to give up. Heaven knows, he had been attempting to rid his mind of her since the assembly and had failed miserably.

"In fact, I was surprised by her refusal of him."

Darcy fidgeted uneasily, and his eyes shifted of their own accord to Richard. One did not air such information in front of a gentleman he had just met.

Mr. Bennet paused and looked at Richard. "This information goes no further than here."

"I shall not repeat a word."

"I would not have my Lizzy's name tarnished."

"I understand," Richard assured him.

Mr. Bennet smiled. "I thought you might as I am given to understand you have a young lady partially under your care." Then, he turned back to Darcy. "All is well, now," he said softly. "You may stop worrying about my loose lips."

"I was not…"

Mr. Bennet snorted. "As I was saying, I thought my Lizzy a good match for Newell, but after speaking to her, I can understand why she would not accept him." His brow furrowed. "She will have a difficult time finding what she wants, however, as there are few as smart as my Lizzy." He smiled. "But that is neither here nor there. What is important is that my wife thinks things might be easier for Elizabeth if there are other gentlemen in the sitting room on a daily basis."

"You wish us to be a sort of buffer between this Newell fellow and your daughter?" Richard asked.

"My wife does. I think it unnecessary since I am certain my daughter can handle herself admirably with just her sisters' help. However, I am also a man who likes his peace, and so I am asking that you visit us at least once next week when Newell is at Longbourn."

Bingley readily assured Mr. Bennet that they would be happy to help him with his dilemma.

With that assurance, Mr. Bennet took his leave, and Darcy returned to the window.

"It seems Mrs. Bennet is not the sort to force a match if her daughter is unhappy with it," Richard said.

Darcy shook his head. "I have more money than Newell."

"Is that truly the reason?" Richard asked.

"What else could it be?"

"Perhaps her daughter prefers you to Newell," Bingley replied.

If only she did. Darcy shook his head. Was that truly what he wanted?

"Does she?" Richard asked.

"No, she does not. She tolerates me." Darcy scrubbed his face with his hands. Why did that thought unsettle him so? "It is understandable, considering the first impression I made."

"Ah, right. She is the lady from the assembly."

Darcy nodded. Elizabeth was, indeed, the fascinating and excessively tempting lady from the assembly, who tortured him by invading his thoughts at every turn. She was the one which he both wished to remove from his mind and desired to cling to as if she were his only means of survival. He rested against the wall of the alcove that the window created in Netherfield's thick outer walls.

Leaning his head back, he closed his eyes as he expelled a great breath. "Mrs. Bennet might be right."

"About what?" Richard asked.

"About a gentleman not knowing he is looking for a wife until he finds her."

There was no denying it, and likely no escaping it. He wished to discover more about Miss Elizabeth Bennet because he was nearly certain she was the lady whom he wished to marry.

Chapter 11

Elizabeth approached Lucas Lodge with a strange sense of trepidation. This was not a place where she was unaccustomed to being entertained. She had been to many dinner parties here, and she had spent many hours visiting with Charlotte in one or another of the rooms in the house. There was, as a matter of fact, a well-worn path between Longbourn and Lucas Lodge, and it was not only Elizabeth who had created that path. Her sisters and her mother made use of it on a regular basis, and servants carried messages back and forth more often than they likely wished to do. However, tonight, the thought of mingling with a company of her neighbours within these walls was not as enticing a thought as it normally was.

Entering the hall, she unfastened her wrap

and, upon removing it, handed it to a waiting maid.

"You are here!" Maria Lucas pushed through those in the entry to where Lydia and Kitty stood. "You must come and help me find some music for later."

"Will there be dancing?" Kitty asked eagerly.

"When does my father not insist upon allowing us to dance?" Maria said with a laugh. "And," she lowered her voice to a loud whisper, "there will be officers."

This comment was met with a small and, Elizabeth had to admit, contained squeal of delight from Lydia.

Closing her eyes, Elizabeth sent a plea heavenward that her youngest sisters would show some restraint tonight. She was in no frame of mind to tolerate comments or looks of disdain from either the ladies or a particular gentleman from Netherfield.

Mama had impressed upon Lydia and Kitty the need to present Jane in the best light. Hopefully, their romantic fancies and eagerness to attend a wedding would help keep them in check. If not that, then perhaps Mama's threat of no ribbons for a month would do the trick – if Lydia and Kitty could remember such lectures when faced with the delightful prospect of officers and dancing.

"Eliza." Charlotte slipped an arm through Elizabeth's. "Mary." She waved her free hand in Mary's direction, motioning for her to join them. "Come. We must make a circuit of the drawing room."

"We must?" Mary asked dryly.

"Would you rather stay with Jane and be pushed forward by your mother?" Charlotte hissed. "If I had three arms, I would rescue Jane as well, though I doubt it is possible. Your mother does seem quite intent upon having Jane at her side."

"Yes, poor Jane," Elizabeth agreed. "But I do not think Jane minds it so overly much tonight as there is only one gentleman whom Mama wishes to see matched with Jane."

"And is Jane delighted by this gentleman as much as your mother is?"

"Have you not seen how much she likes Mr.

Bingley?" Elizabeth asked in surprise. "Do you not remember the assembly?"

"I have, and I do," Charlotte said, "but this is Jane. What one sees is not always what is."

"She is utterly smitten," Mary said. "If Mr. Bingley does not offer for her or, at least, seek a courtship soon, I think she will be crushed."

"She likes him that much?" Charlotte looked for confirmation to Elizabeth who nodded. "Oh, I am glad I was not mistaken in my observations of her. Will it not be a pleasant thing for one of us to finally find a happy situation?"

"Indeed, it will," Mary agreed.

"And who shall be next?" Charlotte whispered in a conspiratorial tone.

"Will Mr. Reed be here?" Elizabeth asked.

Charlotte sighed. "No, but Mr. Darcy will be."

"As will Mr. Newell," Elizabeth retorted. "In fact, he is here now."

"And watching you, Lizzy," Mary added.

"Did you not refuse him?" Charlotte asked in surprise.

"I did, but he thinks he can sway me."

Mr. Newell had been very attentive to her since his arrival on Sunday.

"And is your mother still trying to persuade him to consider you, Mary?" Charlotte asked.

"Yes," Mary said with a sigh.

"Well," Charlotte said as she took a seat on a sofa between Mary and Elizabeth, "we have a muddle of men to sort out, do we not? Who would have thought we would ever be in such a predicament!" She laughed along with Elizabeth and Mary.

"Are you favourably inclined to accepting an officer?" she asked Mary. "The militia is at our doorstep, delivering its bounty of young unattached men – some who have tidy sums and proper houses awaiting them when they have completed their duty to the crown."

"I am not opposed to any gentleman of good character who captures my attention," Mary answered.

"And you, Eliza, have you considered Mr. Darcy as you promised?"

"Have you considered Mr. Newell?" Elizabeth

retorted. She doubted it was so much as she had been thinking about Mr. Darcy.

"I have, and I have determined we will not suit." Charlotte held up a hand to forestall any protest. "I realize that he presents a very secure future and quite likely a content one." She sighed. "However, I cannot give up on Mr. Reed just yet. My heart will not allow it."

"Then, what are we to do with him?" Mary asked.

Charlotte glanced between her two companions and shrugged. "Miss Bingley? That is unless Elizabeth still wishes to match her with Mr. Darcy."

Elizabeth looked toward the door to see the very gentleman about whom they were speaking enter the room with his cousin Colonel Fitzwilliam, the Bingleys, and the Hursts. Heavens! He cut a very handsome and noble figure. He looked her direction, and she found herself smiling without meaning to do so.

"I do not know what I want," she whispered to Charlotte and Mary, though she had to admit the idea of inspiring Mr. Darcy's affection was not as off-putting as it had once been.

"If you were not staring at him and smiling as you are, I might believe you," Charlotte replied. "Shall we greet the new arrivals?"

Mary stood first.

"I have not yet met Mr. Darcy's cousin," Charlotte said. "Father has, of course."

Sir William took it as his duty to greet all the newest arrivals in the area as soon as possible after their arrival, and it was not a duty which he took lightly. His adherence to his duty increased when the new arrival was both a single young gentleman in possession of a fortune and proper connections. Such a fellow would present him with both the prospect of an agreeable hunting partner and a possible match for one of his two daughters.

"Colonel Fitzwilliam," Sir William reached the man before Charlotte, Elizabeth, and Mary, "I would like to introduce you to my eldest daughter. Her sister, Maria, is at the piano, just there." He looked to the far end of the room and back. "May I?"

"Yes, of course," the colonel replied.

"Excellent." Sir William's chest puffed out just a bit more. He was given to airs of importance due to the Sir attached to his name. "This is my daughter, Charlotte. Charlotte, this is Colonel Fitzwilliam, Mr. Darcy's cousin and the Earl of Matlock's son."

Charlotte dipped a curtsey and offered her greeting, which was returned.

"Do you know the Miss Bennets?"

"I do," the colonel answered. "I joined Mr. Bingley yesterday when he called at Longbourn."

"Ah, yes, I have heard that Mr. Bingley has made it a practice to call at Longbourn nearly every day."

"Indeed, he has," Darcy agreed.

"I should not say it, but we are hopeful." Sir William pressed his lips together for a moment before turning the subject. "Have you met Colonel Forster?"

"I have not yet had the pleasure," Colonel Fitzwilliam said, "but I am certain I shall later."

"Undoubtedly," Sir William agreed. "He is a

capital good fellow. I dare say you will not be disappointed. He is soon to be married, I hear – or such is the hope of the gentleman." He paused as if waiting for the colonel to respond in some fashion, but when no response came, he continued, "Are you so fortunate as he?"

Elizabeth felt Charlotte's grip tighten on her arm and could not help but sympathize with her friend. Having a parent who was so forward with questions and who had a bent toward matchmaking was not pleasant for anyone.

"I am more fortunate," Colonel Fitzwilliam said with a crooked grin.

"Are you married?" Sir William asked with no little amount of surprise.

"No, indeed, I am not. I am exceptionally fortunate to find myself unattached in either attachment or inclination to be attached."

Beside her, Charlotte covered a burst of laughter with a cough.

"I do not see how that is more fortunate," Sir William said, oblivious to his daughter's amusement at the comment.

"I may end up returning to the continent or be

sent to the colonies at any moment. It is better to be beholden to no one but my family."

"I can see that point," Sir William acquiesced. "But eventually, you will need to marry."

Colonel Fitzwilliam shook his head. "Not necessarily. If my brother marries and produces an heir, then I really do not need to marry and can take my ease and do as I please."

"But would that not be a lonely existence, sir?" Sir William seemed unable to comprehend such a thing as a gentleman being happy without a wife.

"It does not have to be," the colonel replied with an easy smile. "And I am not beyond being persuaded into the married state if the lady has the right inducements. The requirements of a poor second son and all, you know."

Elizabeth could not contain her laughter at such a thought as the son of an earl being poor.

"Have I misspoken, Miss Elizabeth?" he asked.

"You have, I fear, a lofty definition of the word *poor*."

Colonel Fitzwilliam's smile broadened, and beside him, his cousin chuckled.

Elizabeth liked the way Mr. Darcy's features softened and his eyes sparkled with amusement when in the presence of Colonel Fitzwilliam.

It had been the same when he and Colonel Fitzwilliam had called at Longbourn. Mr. Darcy seemed to enjoy allowing his cousin to take the lead in a conversation so that he could simply enjoy whatever might unfold.

Seeing him at ease caused Elizabeth to desire to know more of that gentleman – the one who laughed and teased and rolled his eyes at foolishness. However, at present, she would have to satisfy herself with becoming better acquainted with his cousin, and so, she turned her eyes from Mr. Darcy and back to Colonel Fitzwilliam.

"Is it not a term relative to what one is accustomed?" Colonel Fitzwilliam asked her.

Elizabeth shook her head. "No, I believe it is a term which is more absolute in its meaning."

"I cannot agree," he retorted. "However, I will allow that my definition of poor is not as destitute of some comforts as it is for many others."

"Have you been witness to such suffering, Colonel?" Charlotte asked.

Colonel Fitzwilliam sobered. "Indeed, I have, Miss Lucas."

The light which had been in Mr. Darcy's eyes faded and a furrow formed between his eyebrows. Elizabeth could only imagine the worry one would have for a loved one who had been or might be called to face the atrocities of war.

"And yet you speak so lightly of want?"

Charlotte could be as bad as Mary sometimes! Why must she pursue this course of conversation? Could she not see that Mr. Darcy was not comfortable with it?

Colonel Fitzwilliam cocked a brow. "My tone in this discussion – in this setting – does not negate my understanding of the seriousness of the plight of many both here in England and on the continent where war has ravaged homes and families. I have lived amongst the squalor and stench of such places. They are not just something I pontificate about from a comfortable home as some do." His eyes roamed the room as if indicating that this was the comfortable home of which he spoke.

Charlotte merely smiled and said, "I am glad to hear it."

"Nor do I normally speak about such thing with ladies," the colonel added.

"I am certain that is a very good practice to have, Colonel," Sir William said quickly, addressing his daughter, as he shifted uneasily.

Anyone who knew Charlotte knew that she was not fond of being dismissed based solely on the fact that she was a lady, especially if the topic at hand was one about which Charlotte thought it a lady's duty to be informed, and the plight of the less fortunate was, according to Charlotte, firmly entrenched in a lady's domain. Was it not ladies who called on their poor neighbors and tenants?

Elizabeth understood very well why Charlotte's father was eager to turn the subject quickly.

"Perhaps you could help your sister decide which pieces of music would be best for performance and dancing, my dear." Sir William continued, turning to Mr. Darcy and Colonel Fitzwilliam. "Are there any songs which you would like to hear? Charlotte would be happy to take your recommendations to her sister."

"I do not have any. Do you, Darcy?"

"No," Darcy replied and then, turning his attention to Elizabeth, added, "May we escort you to your sisters?"

Elizabeth placed her hand on his outstretched arm. "I would like that very much, Mr. Darcy," she said, and while her mind told her in tones of a screeching hawk that being so welcoming would surely be shared by Sir William with her mother before five minutes had passed, something much quieter and calmer, somewhere in the vicinity of her heart, firmly instructed her mind to hold its peace.

Chapter 12

Mr. Newell, with Caroline on his arm, nudged his way into the group of people looking through music near the piano at the far end of the drawing room.

"You will sing for us, will you not, Elizabeth?" Mr. Newell asked.

Darcy nearly growled at the familiar way in which Newell addressed Elizabeth. It was one thing to be so informal at the lady's home or in her garden, but to do so in a social setting, even if it was among friends, was, in Darcy's way of thinking, completely improper.

"Oh, yes, Miss Elizabeth, you must," Caroline agreed. "I have heard so much about your talent that I would dearly love to experience it." She took a seat next to Elizabeth.

"I do not think tonight is that sort of evening," Elizabeth deferred.

"I will ask Sir William," Newell offered.

Had the man not yet learned that Elizabeth did not like to be pushed to do things?

"Please, do not," Elizabeth said with some force.

"But I am certain Mr. Darcy would also love to hear you sing," Caroline said with a flutter of lashes for Darcy.

She had been teasing him about his upcoming nuptials for two days now – ever since he refused to go for a walk with her and Louisa because he was going to Longbourn. That coupled with his inability to tolerate her barbs about Netherfield's neighbors had put in her mind that he was as good as betrothed to Elizabeth, and that was not an idea which she could bear with any kind of equanimity.

She was right, of course, Darcy had lost his heart to Elizabeth. However, he was not willing to share such information publicly, nor was he willing to put upon that lady to sing when she did not wish to do so.

"I fear you are mistaken," Darcy said.

"What?" Caroline cried in mock horror. "Do you hear him, Miss Elizabeth? He has no faith in your performance."

"You are still mistaken," Darcy said. "I have no desire to persuade a lady to perform against her wishes. That has nothing to do with whether or not I wish to hear Miss Elizabeth sing."

"Then, you do wish to hear her?" Again, Caroline fluttered her lashes and smirked.

"I would not forego the opportunity if it was presented, but only if it is what the lady wishes."

"Thank you," Elizabeth said. "I am not fond of performing, especially in such a large group, as Mr. Newell knows very well."

If the man was attempting to convince Elizabeth to reconsider his offer, he was doing a deplorable job of it.

"I do wish Miss Darcy was here," Caroline said as she looked on while Elizabeth turned pages in a book of music. "She plays so well and is so willing to entertain."

"She has only ever played for family and close friends." Darcy knew exactly what Caroline was attempting to do, and he'd be hanged if he was going to allow her to make Elizabeth feel inferior.

"Are not these good friends of the Bennets? I had thought everyone knew everyone in Meryton. Is that not how it is in these country villages?"

"No," Charlotte said, "that is not how it is. My father is very sociable and will mingle with friends of long-standing right alongside those who are new to our community such as yourself, Colonel Fitzwilliam, and the militia. However, if you would like to perform, I could ask my father if he has time in the schedule for such a thing."

"Surely, you are not saying that your father is the designer of tonight's festivities, are you?"

"I am," Charlotte replied. "My mother sees to the menus while my father plans the entertainment. They work very well together, and I have yet to meet a person who has not enjoyed him or herself at one of their soirees."

"But entertainment is the lady of the house's domain," Caroline protested.

"It still is here," Charlotte said with a smile. "It

is just that the lady of the house deigns to bow to her husband's desire to be part of the planning."

Elizabeth's lips were tipped up in a smile, but she applied herself diligently to the book on her lap, doing no more to engage in the debate than to cast an amused look at her friend.

She was delightful even in her restraint. Was there a lady who was ever more well-suited to him than she was?

"Why do you not sing, Mr. Newell?" Mary asked. "If there are to be vocal displays, I would think you would wish to be part of it. Perhaps, you and Miss Bingley could even sing a duet. Would that not be lovely, Lydia?"

Lydia turned wide eyes to her sister. "Yes?"

Richard chuckled. "You do not sound very convinced, Miss Lydia."

Lydia's face flushed. "I am not entirely certain what I am agreeing to. I was not paying attention." Her eyes wandered back to the group of officers who were standing nearby.

"Your sister thought a duet between Miss Bingley and Mr. Newell was something we all might enjoy," Richard said.

"Oh! I do not know how well Miss Bingley sings, but Simon is quite good," Lydia agreed. Then, she looked at Maria. "Is there to be singing? I thought we were only dancing."

Maria looked as horrified as any young lady might at the idea of singing taking place when dancing should. "I do not think we will have time for both." Then, her brow furrowed. "Do you think any of the officers sing?"

Richard chuckled. "I am certain they do, but whether they do so well or know songs appropriate to our audience is the true question."

"What do you mean?" Maria asked.

"He means that it is best if we forego the singing," Charlotte said with a pointed look for Richard.

And that was the end of the discussion of singing. Soon after, all the songs needed for dancing had been selected. Charlotte, Mary, Elizabeth, and Caroline had been enlisted to play since it seemed the fairest way to do it according to Miss Lydia. This way, no lady would have to miss all the dancing.

Mr. Newell had left during this discussion and

returned just as it was concluded. "I have checked, and there is just enough time for us all to take a walk in the garden before our meal. And," he smiled at Lydia and Maria, "I have brought some new friends to meet you. I asked your fathers if I could present these officers to you now so that when it was time to dance, everyone will know each other."

"Oh, how clever!" Kitty cried before Newell set about the task of introducing the three officers – Mr. Denny, Mr. Saunders, and Captain Carter.

"Now, Elizabeth," Newell held out his hand to her, "shall we walk before we eat?"

"Would you not rather stroll with someone else?" she asked.

"No, I would not."

A small scowl passed across her expression, and then with a glance in Darcy's direction with what he thought was a look of regret, she placed her hand in Mr. Newell's.

"Charlotte and I will walk with you," Mary said, rising quickly to join Elizabeth.

"Richard," Darcy said, "do you wish to walk in the garden?"

His cousin shrugged. "So long as I do not have to hold your arm."

Darcy chuckled. "I would not expect you to do so."

"Miss Bingley, will you be joining us?" Richard asked with an outstretched hand.

Darcy would have to thank him for his service later. While he might still have to walk on one side of Caroline and allow her to hold his arm, he would not have to walk with her alone. It was surprising how much had changed for him since arriving in Hertfordshire. In two short weeks, he had gone from considering Caroline as the lady who would walk by his side for the remainder of his life to wishing her to be anywhere but attached to his arm. The lady he wished to accompany him on all his walks was glancing over her shoulder at him.

He would speak to her tomorrow to see if there was any possibility of progressing from friend to something more. He would not offer anything. He would merely present the idea of such a thing, and if she seemed hesitant, he would assure her that they would remain friends. And then – he smiled to himself – he would begin in earnest to win her, but not as Newell did by attempting to push her forward and claiming her without seeking her permission. No, he would sway her with kindness, friendship, and respect.

Ahead of his party of three, Mary was looking back at him with an uneasy expression. Something was not right.

"Will you excuse me," he said to his companions. "I think Miss Mary would like to speak with me about something."

Reluctantly, Caroline released her hold of his arm.

"May I be of service?" Darcy asked when he reached Charlotte and Mary.

"Just listen," Mary said.

He discreetly pointed to Elizabeth and Newell. "To them?" he whispered.

"Yes."

"Why?" It seemed an odd thing to be asked to eavesdrop.

"Do you know a Mr. Wickham?"

Darcy's blood ran cold at Charlotte's question.

"I do." How had that name arrived in Hertfordshire? Was there nowhere Darcy could go where he would be free of that wastrel?

"I do not believe it." Elizabeth's tone was adamant.

"You have only known him for two weeks. There is much you do not yet know about Mr. Darcy. He is a private man and perhaps for a good reason. Mr. Denny," Newell called.

"I simply cannot believe that he could be so bad."

"What are you saying, Newell?" Darcy left Mary and Charlotte to approach the man. There was no way he was going to simply listen to himself be disparaged.

"Oh, Mr. Darcy." Newell greeted him with a cunning smile. "I had not expected you to join us."

That was obvious.

"What are you saying?" Anger at being the topic of gossip mingled with the fury that the mere mention of Wickham's name always conjured, and Darcy's question came out more like a growl than a demand.

"I was simply cautioning Elizabeth about accepting new friends too easily."

"Do you not think she is able to think for herself? Is this why you are constantly attempting to tell her what she should or should not do? Perhaps you should caution her about keeping old acquaintances."

"I have not disregarded my father's will to the harm of another."

Darcy's heart pounded, and his breathing became pronounced. Keeping his emotions in regulation was nearly impossible when faced with the lies Wickham liked to spread about Darcy.

"Neither did I," he ground out through clenched teeth.

Elizabeth was eying him warily.

"I do not know what Mr. Newell has told you, but if he is speaking of Wickham," he spat the name, "I can assure you that it is a lie."

Newell shrugged as Denny joined him. "Mr.

Denny, did you not tell me that Mr. Wickham was supposed to receive a living but did not because Mr. Darcy refused to give it to him?"

Denny's eyes shifted uneasily from Newell to Darcy and back. "That is what Wickham told me."

"And how do you know Mr. Wickham?" Newell asked.

"We have been friends since Cambridge."

Darcy's lips twisted into a snarl. "How good of you not to say you attended Cambridge together, since I know Wickham attended very few classes and spent most of his time on other less noble pursuits."

"What gentleman does not have some fun when he is in university?" Newell countered.

"Do you know Wickham?" Darcy asked him.

"No, I only know what Denny has told me."

"And I hope for your sake, Mr. Denny, that you only know what that liar has told you and that you are not misleading others on purpose." Darcy's chest rose and fell rapidly.

"Did you refuse to give Mr. Wickham a living?" Newell asked.

"Yes, but it is not as you suppose."

"Then, tell us how it is."

Darcy looked around the gathered group. "I cannot. Not here." There were innocent young ladies present who did not need to hear about Wickham's proclivities. "Suffice it to say he was not fit for the church."

"You decided that?" Elizabeth asked.

"His actions did."

"But if it is what your father wanted..."

"My father did not know the half of what Wickham did."

"And this is the sort of gentleman you would choose over me?" Newell asked. "A gentleman who finds you only tolerable and treats those he has known for his entire life so shabbily just because his father favoured Mr. Wickham over him. A gentleman who decides who is and is not worthy of an inheritance? Will you still choose him? Or will you choose me? My offer still stands, Elizabeth."

Elizabeth looked from Newell to Darcy and back. "Do you think that I must choose one of you or be a spinster?"

"No, no, no," Newell said quickly. "I just think you need to consider what you are doing."

"You idiot!" Darcy shouted, and then, he allowed his anger to make contact with Newell's chin by way of his fist, sending Newell staggering. "She is far more capable of thinking than you are."

"Mr. Darcy!" Elizabeth cried, grasping his arm before he could hit Newell again.

"He treats you like a child – telling you what you should do and not listening to what you want. Is that for what you wish?"

Elizabeth shook her head while her brow furrowed as if she could not believe what was happening. "No, it is not. Nor do I wish to be attached to a hard man who cannot regulate his actions."

"He has lied to you about me!" Darcy shouted.

"Who will it be, Elizabeth?" Newell said.

Elizabeth crossed her arms and glared first at Newell and then Darcy. "Neither of you. I want nothing to do with either of you."

She clamped her lips closed and turned to her friend. "Charlotte, please see that my things get sent home, and Mary, tell our mother that I am not feeling well."

She stepped closer to Darcy and lowered her voice. "And I nearly thought you were a proper gentleman. How foolish I have been."

"Elizabeth, please," Darcy begged.

She held up her hand to keep him from speaking further. "Leave me be."

And with that, she took her leave of the garden and Lucas Lodge.

"Give her time," Charlotte whispered to him. "She is overwrought. Just give her time."

Darcy nodded for he felt as if his ability to speak had been taken from him with Elizabeth's departure.

"Darcy?" Richard clapped him on the shoulder. "What do you need?"

"Home." He needed to be home – not at Netherfield but either town or Pemberley. He would give her all the time she needed, and with any luck, in the process, he would reclaim his heart and find a way to move on without her.

Chapter 13

"Elizabeth," Mr. Bennet called through her bedroom door as he knocked. "Elizabeth, may I enter?"

Elizabeth groaned and lifted her head. "Yes," she answered before burying her face in her pillows once again. She had arrived home from Lucas Lodge, gone straight to her room, and thrown herself face-first onto her bed where, for the past quarter-hour, for some inexplicable reason, she had done nothing but weep into her pillows.

She was angry. That was a fact that could not be denied. However, her anger had been somewhat spent in an aggressive walk, punctuated with loud and improper language. Her mother would remove every book from Elizabeth's room if she had heard some of the things which her daughter had said.

The door opened a crack.

"I have not come alone," her father's voice carried from the hall to her bed. "Mr. Bingley is with me."

Mr. Bingley? Elizabeth popped up and looked toward her father. Surely, her father was not going to bring Mr. Bingley into her bedchamber.

"He insisted that he be allowed to talk to you."

Elizabeth rubbed at her tear-dampened face and then smoothed her dress as she rose from her bed. She opened her mouth to say something – anything – but nothing came out, for when her father opened her bedroom door completely, there, standing behind him, was Mr. Bingley.

"Miss Elizabeth." Mr. Bingley took two steps inside her room and stopped.

"A bit further, my boy, so I can close the door."

Mr. Bingley followed Mr. Bennet's directions and then began again. "Miss Elizabeth, I could not allow you to be misled about my friend." He took two more steps in her direction. "Darcy is every inch a gentleman. I will give you that he is often a bit above himself and that he can have a surly temper when pushed past his limits." Mr. Bingley smiled. "I know that very well, for I have pushed him past his limits many, many times."

Mr. Bennet chuckled, and Elizabeth could not help but feel a little amused. Mr. Bingley was contagiously amiable.

"However, tonight, he was not pushed beyond his limits on his own behalf."

Elizabeth's brow furrowed. "Was he not?"

Mr. Bingley shook his head. "His actions and words were prompted by his care for his sister and..." He paused and smiled sadly. "You."

Elizabeth's eyebrows rose over surprised eyes. Mr. Darcy cared for her? Had she heard Mr. Bingley correctly?

"I understand from Mary," Mr. Bennet inserted before Mr. Bingley could continue, "that Mr. Newell stepped well-past his bounds in attempting to sway your opinion." He shook his head. "I had thought him smarter than to attempt to coerce you into reversing your decision. I would not abide such behaviour toward any of my daughters. However, I truly thought he understood that such tactics would not work in his favour where you are concerned. He leaves at first light, and that is only because I refused to allow your mother to turn him out in the dead of night."

He chuckled as Elizabeth's eyes grew wide, and she blinked. "No one offends one of Mrs. Bennet's daughters without paying their dues." He chuckled some more. "She was crowing about how proud she was of Mr. Darcy for defending her daughter when I left her in your sisters' care. Your youngest sisters will not be pleased, I suppose, since she has declared the officers wholly unsuitable."

"Mama?" Her mother supported Mr. Darcy and discredited handsome young gentlemen in smart red coats? Elizabeth glanced toward her window to make certain the moon was still rising and that the whole of nature had not been turned on its head by the sun's returning to take the moon's place. No, everything seemed to be as it should be outside her window. Elizabeth sank down to sit on the edge of her bed for things seemed most certainly out of sort inside her room and her mind.

"Yes, my dear, your mother wishes to see you all well-matched, but she will not promote a match where she suspects ignoble intentions. She thinks rather highly of her daughters. As she should, I might add."

"I could not agree more," Mr. Bingley inserted.

Mr. Bennet clapped him on the shoulder. "I should hope you do. Now, carry on. I think Elizabeth is bright enough to conclude that Mr. Darcy's actions toward Mr. Newell were because Mr. Newell was just what Mr. Darcy said he was – an idiot –" He held his daughter's gaze and added pointedly, "to you."

Elizabeth's hand rose to cover her heart and rub away the pricking pain she felt there.

"What Mr. Denny said was true but only to a point," Mr. Bingley began. "Mr. Wickham was favoured by Mr. Darcy's father, and he was left a living in the elder Mr. Darcy's will. However, what was not said, and is likely unknown by Mr.

Denny, is that Mr. Wickham refused the living and received a sum of money in its place. That money was quickly wasted in wild living. He then returned to collect the living. Darcy knew Mr. Wickham's proclivities. He knew that Mr. Wickham was not designed for the church, and he had already given him money in place of the living. Therefore, he refused to install Mr. Wickham in the position that had fallen open."

"Oh." The word was expelled on a breath that carried with it a great deal of the contempt Elizabeth had felt toward Mr. Darcy, leaving a hole to be filled with the first harbingers of remorse and allowing something else to hang once again at the edges of her mind. It was that same unsettled feeling she had felt for some days now, the one which made her feel as if a wonderful surprise was just within her reach if only she would look for it.

"Mr. Wickham was not happy with Darcy's decision and spoke very cruelly about him. But that was not all he did."

The remorse Elizabeth had begun to feel grew, pushed forward by a sense of dread about what

Mr. Bingley would say next and puffed up by that other odd feeling. Why did she feel as if whatever happiness this strange feeling had promised was about to be torn from her?

"I cannot tell you more than that, other than to say that, recently, Mr. Wickham misused Miss Darcy's heart in a most grievous fashion."

"Oh, do not tell me Mr. Darcy has lost his sister!" Elizabeth cried. Emotions tumbled and clashed within her, causing her stomach to roil and tears to threaten once again.

Mr. Bingley shook his head. "Wickham was not entirely successful."

Elizabeth sighed in relief, though she still could not push aside the urge to cry at some great loss.

"If he had been successful, his destruction of Darcy would have been complete. That is why it was beyond Darcy's ability to keep his emotions in good regulation. This history with Wickham and Miss Darcy is also why Darcy could not explain himself."

The tears could be contained no longer. As they fell, the sense of loss did not diminish. If anything, it increased. How stupid she had been to assume the worst of Mr. Darcy without giving him time to defend himself.

Mr. Bingley pressed his handkerchief into Elizabeth's hand and knelt before her where she sat on the edge of her bed.

"Darcy is every inch a gentleman," Mr. Bingley whispered.

Elizabeth nodded her agreement. He was. He truly was. And she had condemned him.

"I did not wish to overset you," Mr. Bingley continued. "However, you needed to know."

"Thank you," Elizabeth whispered. She was glad to know the truth even if in learning it, it had revealed her own dreadful behaviour.

"I hope my friend is as forgiving of my sharing of this information as you are grateful," Mr. Bingley quipped, causing Elizabeth to smile through her tears. "Perhaps you and your sisters could call at Netherfield tomorrow?"

"Of course," Elizabeth agreed. She must attempt to make amends — if Mr. Darcy would see her. The thought of him sending her away threatened to cause a fresh round of tears, but with a deep and steady breath, she managed to stave them off for the time being.

"Capital." Mr. Bingley rose. "I shall return to Lucas Lodge then and assure your mother and sisters that all is well, for I know it will be."

With all her heart, Elizabeth wished that Mr. Bingley's declaration was true and that all would indeed be well, but she knew that no matter how much she wished for it or Mr. Bingley believed it, all might not be well. She had injured a gentleman who was already reeling from a previous blow.

"I will remain at home," Mr. Bennet said. "Just in case Simon returns before the others." He placed a hand on Elizabeth's shoulder. "You do not know how much it grieves me that he has behaved as he has – although, knowing the prize that you are, I find I can understand his desperation not to lose you."

"Papa."

"No, Lizzy, it is true." He bent and kissed the top of her head. "I will send up some food and your maid to see that you are properly tucked into bed without an empty stomach."

"Thank you, Papa." She caught his hand and squeezed it.

He had always cared so well for her and her sisters – at least, to a point. He struggled to know how to relate to his youngest children, but then, he and she had also had their times when they had not gotten on so well as they presently did.

She sat just as she was on the edge of her bed contemplating her father and then, Mr. Darcy – another gentleman who, according to his friend, cared for her – until her maid arrived to scold her with an "oh, miss," for the soiled state of her slippers, stockings, and skirts.

However, the state of her clothing was not nearly so tragic as the state of her heart, for she was beginning to suspect that the unsettling feeling that had lifted her spirits and brought an excitement to greeting each new day was, in reality, an attachment and fondness for the gentleman she had so grievously injured.

~*~*~

"He left me a written apology," Elizabeth said, the next morning, in answer to Charlotte's question about how Mr. Newell had taken his leave from her. "I refused to leave my room until he had left."

She would likely have to see him again at some point. Their families were friends. However, time and distance from last night might make their next meeting one which she could tolerate with some amount of equanimity.

"And I read it before it was given to her," Mary added. "Just in case she decided to cast it into the fire without opening it."

"You have very little faith in me," Elizabeth said with a laugh.

"Oh, no! We have a great deal of faith in your temper, Eliza." Charlotte wound her arm around Elizabeth's as they walked toward Netherfield.

"Do not say you did not consider burning it. I will not believe you if you do because I know I would have considered burning it instead of reading it," Jane said.

Mary, Charlotte, and Elizabeth all ceased walking and stared at Jane.

"What?" Jane asked. "He was horrid to you. It would have been perfectly justified." Her brow furrowed as her lips pursed. "I am not above being angry, and what Simon did made me angry. I was so relieved when Mr. Bingley returned and told me that you were well."

Jane had shared that fact with Elizabeth at least three times since she had arrived home last night. Apparently, Mr. Bingley had worked a bit of magic when he returned to Lucas Lodge last evening, for Elizabeth had not been scolded at all by their mother. In fact, she had gone on and on about how lovely the evening had been – except for that one little mishap when Mr. Darcy defended her daughter, of course.

The food had nearly been as good as she herself would have served. However, the cook at Lucas Lodge was not so skilled as the cook at Longbourn.

The music had been delightful, and she had even danced herself. Mr. Bingley had insisted on it, and she simply could not refuse. However, she was nearly certain the piano at Lucas Lodge needed to be tuned for it did not sound quite the same as the one at Longbourn did.

The wine had been a good vintage, but Longbourn's cellars were better-stocked thanks to her brother Gardener.

The list had gone on and on, with every item being praised as nearly as excellent as it would have been if she had hosted the event herself, and an event hosted by Mrs. Bennet was to what Elizabeth's mother's litany of accolades had led. It was not something that would be put off either. Mrs. Bennet had no desire to wait too long to host her own soiree, which was why Jane carried, in her reticule, an invitation for the residents of Netherfield to come to dinner next week.

Charlotte, who had come to call on Elizabeth and see for herself that her friend was well, also carried an invitation, which she would give to her mother once she returned home.

"I wish the carriage had been available," Mary said with a glance at the sky.

The grey clouds which had been in the distance when they began their walk to Netherfield were no longer all that distant. In fact, they were nearly overhead.

"I told Mama that the breeze was too strong for the rain to stay away for long."

"We have umbrellas," Charlotte said.

"We will still be a sight when we arrive with our petticoats and boots covered in mud. You know how these roads can be," Mary grumbled.

"We will do our best to stay clean," Jane assured her.

"Perhaps if we walk a bit faster," Elizabeth suggested. "Netherfield is not that much further now – maybe a quarter-hour if we do not dawdle."

"I am not dawdling," Mary snapped. "You know how my hair gets when I walk in the rain."

Poor Mary had been blessed with hair that curled easily and hung in waves without an ounce of work aside from brushing it. However, wet weather was not Mary's friend. Even now, her hair was beginning to look unkempt as it began to puff because of the moisture in the air.

"I have a comb," Jane assured her. "We can ask if there is a place to refresh ourselves after entering. I am certain no one would mind one bit, especially if it is raining."

"I just do not want to walk in the rain," Mary grumbled.

And as if provoked to cause mischief by Mary's comment, the cloud overhead began to release its watery cargo.

Chapter 14

"Could you please do whatever it is you need to do more rapidly," Darcy grumbled at Richard. "Or, you may find yourself riding your horse in the rain."

Darcy's things had been ready and tied onto the carriage for over an hour already. It was only his cousin's not being prepared to leave which was delaying his escape.

"I had hoped to start our journey before the rain began."

"Find a book and make yourself comfortable. I will only be half an hour at most with Bingley. It is not as if I can leave wherever I am and whatever I am doing whenever I want and come calling on the fellow as some can." Richard shot Darcy a displeased look.

Darcy scowled and sank into a chair in the

library. He had no idea why Bingley needed to talk to Richard in private at all. However, he was not in the mood to ferret out the reason.

"Make it a quick half-hour."

He flopped his head back and looked up at the ceiling. He needed to be away from here – from her.

He shook his head. Not a gentleman, indeed! He had been as gentlemanly as he knew how to be! And yet – he swallowed – he had failed. Failed to convince the one lady, whose good opinion mattered most to him, that he was a gentleman in actions as well as title.

"I should have just danced with her," he said to the emptiness of the room as he thought back to the assembly. His lips tipped up in amusement of their own accord as he remembered her refusal of his offer to dance after Bingley had maneuvered things so that an introduction to Elizabeth was impossible to refuse.

He chuckled softly. Bingley was a persistent fellow and a good friend.

Darcy lifted his head up from where it rested on the back of his chair. Meeting Elizabeth and getting to know her, even though their time had been limited, had been a wonderful thing.

If only he had not failed...

"Mr. Darcy?"

Darcy turned his head toward the door. "Can I be of service, Miss Bingley?"

"Will you ever call me Caroline?" she asked as she stepped into the library.

He shook his head. "Likely not."

She sighed. "Then, I truly have no hope?"

"I am sorry, but no."

She crossed the room and sat down near him. "I suspected as much last evening." She looked down at her hands. "I still think I would make a much better mistress of Pemberley than *she* would."

Darcy let the words roll over him. It really did not matter who would or would not make the best mistress of his estate. It was who held his heart which mattered.

Caroline raised her eyes to him. "I did not know Mr. Newell was going to speak to *her* about Mr. Wickham. You know I would never..." Her voice trailed off, and she blew out a breath as if something exceedingly great was troubling her. "You should tell her." She rolled her eyes and once again blew out a breath. "It is not right that she should think of you so meanly – even if she is insignificant."

She slapped her hands on the arms of the chair in which she was sitting and pushed up. "That is all I can do," she muttered.

"Tell her," she said to Darcy before crossing the room quickly.

She turned as she reached the door. "Would you be so kind as to tell my brother of this good deed?"

"Was it required?" Darcy asked in surprise.

She lifted her chin. "I prefer not to say." And with that, she was gone.

Darcy chuckled. Caroline must have been taken to task by her brother for whatever role she had played in last night's scene at Lucas Lodge, which meant that Bingley must be as serious about courting Miss Bennet as he claimed. For, it was a rare thing for Bingley to chastise his sister unless she had crossed some line and posed a hazard to his happiness or presented a source of possible harm to someone close to him.

Rising, Darcy crossed to the window to look out at the gathering grayness. How well the sky reflected his mood.

Tell her.

He let the suggestion roll around his mind. How could he do such a thing? Would he not look pathetic begging a lady who was set against him to consider him because he had been treated ill by another? What sort of fellow allowed his sister to fall into the clutches of a man such as Wickham?

Tell her. The thought repeated itself more loudly.

He rested against the window casing and studied the sky. Could he reveal his greatest failure to Elizabeth? He certainly had a penchant for failing those he loved.

He sucked in a breath. Those he loved? He blew out the breath. If he loved Elizabeth, how could he leave Hertfordshire without, at least, attempting to explain himself?

He turned from the window and hurried out

of the library and to the study where he knocked and then, without waiting for a reply, opened the door and poked his head in.

"You had to see Bingley about a glass of whisky?" he asked in surprise as he took in the scene before him.

Richard cast a look at Bingley. "No, the whisky was just an accompaniment."

"Precisely," Bingley agreed.

"And I do have to travel with you while you are in a state, so drinking a bit before entering the carriage seemed a wise thing to do." Richard shot him a teasing smile. "Now, what brings you here to interrupt us?"

"Pardon me, sir." A footman entered and scooted past Darcy. "A message from –"

"Yes, yes, the one for which I have been waiting," Bingley interrupted as he quickly opened the missive.

"Is everything well?" Richard asked from behind the rim of his glass.

Bingley smiled. "It is as it should be."

"Well, then, I believe our business is concluded, is it not?" Richard asked as he drained the contents from his glass.

"For now," Bingley replied with a smile.

Something did not seem right to Darcy, but to attempt to argue it out of either his cousin or Bingley would only delay him in his purpose.

"I would like to stop at Longbourn," he said to Richard.

"Are you looking to call Newell out?" Richard asked with a laugh.

"No, I intend to tell Miss Elizabeth all I know about George Wickham."

Richard's head tipped. "Is that wise?"

"I have no idea," Darcy replied truthfully. To tell Elizabeth might be an incredibly large mistake or the desperate act he needed to earn himself a second chance to win her. "However, I must. I cannot bear the thought of her not hearing my explanation for my behaviour."

"She would not listen to you last night." Richard motioned for Darcy to exit the study ahead of him. "She may not listen to you today either."

"Then, I will speak to her father or her sisters or even her mother if I must."

He had to make one final attempt to rise above what Elizabeth thought of him. To charge forward and be overcome by the enemy was a failure that paled in comparison to turning tail and seeking refuge in the nearest stronghold until the enemy had passed. One required fortitude and sacrifice. The other required a conscience that could bear the shame of weakness. Darcy's conscience was not designed for such. Wickham had taught him that.

He gathered his greatcoat from the chair in the entry where, in frustration, he had tossed it when Richard had announced he could not leave until he had spoken to Bingley. He did not put it on, however. There would be time to put the thing on in the carriage.

"Thank you for your hospitality, Bingley."

"You will return to us at some point, will you not?"

Darcy nodded. "I believe I will."

"Sooner, rather than later would be my preference," Bingley said.

"If it is possible," Darcy assured him.

If Miss Elizabeth listened to his explanation, he might not be leaving at all. For, if she would listen to him and give him another chance, he would take it — holding fast to it until either he succeeded, or the last remnants of hope were pried from his fingers.

He dashed from the steps to the carriage just as the rain began to fall.

Richard, however, stood a moment longer on the steps, talking to Bingley. The man was exasperating!

Darcy shrugged into his coat while he waited for his cousin to finish with Bingley and then trot to the carriage.

"I'd rather be staying," Richard said as he settled into his seat.

"You were the one who said he needed to get back to town today. You do remember telling me that when you arrived, do you not?"

"Yes, I remember that. However, if you must know the truth, I have no desire to go back to my unit." He looked out the window in the direction of Netherfield. "Bingley has a pleasant situation, does he not?"

"He does."

"I could sell my commission."

Darcy's brow furrowed. "What are you saying?"

Richard shrugged. "I am saying that the idea of a smaller estate and the life it would afford does not seem so dull as I had thought it might be. Netherfield is not far from town, and the land, which Bingley has not leased but could, would be enough to have a profitable existence, do you not think?"

"That is what I told him." He cocked his head and studied his cousin. "Sheep do not carry weapons, and they are not a source of any sort of excitement."

"I have had my fill of excitement."

Darcy was not certain he believed that. "And the income produced would not be grand."

"Be that as it may, it would be enough to enjoy a few months in town, which is not far away, and I hear that the hunting in this area is good, so my practice with a gun would not be for naught."

What was his cousin proposing?

"Has Bingley decided to not keep Netherfield?"

Richard smirked. "He has not decided one way or the other. I am just using Netherfield as an example. Should I be able to find a situation such as he has, I would give it serious contemplation. Father has been pressing me to consider politics for some time." He chuckled. "That should be good for a skirmish and would need some careful strategizing."

"And your father would be willing to send a few pounds your way to see you join him in parliament."

Richard nodded and tapped his nose. "Even if I would be in the lower house."

"Are you certain this is what you would like to do with your life? You were always lining up soldiers and attacking things when we were young. Sheep do not line up or follow orders, and it is very bad practice to order they be flogged for disregarding your directives."

Richard laughed. "There are always the servants."

Darcy's mouth dropped open.

"I jest. I do not believe in flogging servants or sheep." He leaned forward and looked out the window as if he was searching for something. "Say, is that not the Miss Bennets?" he asked Darcy.

"Where?" Darcy leaned forward to look out the window with Richard.

"Just there, in front of us."

"Indeed, I think it is. At least three of them are Miss Bennets. However, the fourth appears to be Miss Lucas."

"You mean the lady with the sharp tongue," Richard muttered.

"She has never been sharp with me," Darcy countered.

Richard refused to reply. Instead, he tapped on the roof of the carriage so that the vehicle would stop. Then, without waiting for a servant to open the door or put the steps in place, Richard opened the door himself and jumped down.

"Ladies," Darcy heard him say as he bowed. "Are you bound for Netherfield?"

"Yes, we are," Mary answered.

"It is fortunate, then, that we have come across you when we have for there is a road just ahead where we can turn around."

There was? How did Richard know that?

"Will you join us?" He held his hand out to Miss Mary first.

"Gladly," she said. "I am not fond of walking in the rain."

"And I am not fond of riding in it, which is why I was travelling to town with Darcy today."

He handed first Miss Mary into the carriage, then, Miss Bennet and Miss Lucas, before, finally, assisting Miss Elizabeth up the steps which had been hurriedly put in place while he was talking.

"You can sit on the far side of Darcy so that my wet coat does not soil your pelisse."

"That is very thoughtful of you, Colonel." She smiled tentatively at Darcy. "Would you rather my sister or Charlotte sit beside you?" she asked softly

He shook his head. There would never be

another lady whom he would wish to have seated beside him rather than her.

"Take the road the old master used to take and return us to Netherfield," Richard said to Darcy's coachman before climbing into the carriage.

"The road the old master used to take?" Darcy questioned.

Richard nodded. "As I have heard it, the old master of Netherfield's wife was a forgetful sort of lady, and she would, without fail, forget something every time they left to go to London."

Miss Lucas laughed. "It was not just when they went to London. She would also forget things when on her way to Meryton."

"Indeed?" Richard said with some curiosity. "Then, the road her husband had put in place was an even greater benefit to him."

"It most certainly was. According to my mother, until he had installed the turnaround, they were forever using the drive at Longbourn," Charlotte said.

"Oh, yes!" Miss Bennet cried. "I remember that, though I was very small when they stopped having to use our drive. Do you remember it, Lizzy?"

"I am afraid I do not."

"I barely recall it at all myself," Miss Bennet assured her sister. She shifted her attention to Darcy. "Your cousin said you were on your way to London. Were you leaving us?"

"I was. However, I was not going to do so without calling at Longbourn." His chest constricted at the admission, and he held his breath as he waited to hear how such news would be welcomed.

"I am happy to hear it," Miss Bennet said with one of her ever-present smiles.

"As am I," he heard whispered softly beside him.

The breath he had been holding whooshed out of him. He had hope. Failure might yet be avoided.

Chapter 15

"Boots and wet coats by the fire!" Mr. Bingley ordered after he had given his hearty welcome to everyone when they entered Netherfield. "And if any of you feel in the least bit chilled, join your clothing."

"We need to talk," Mr. Darcy whispered to Elizabeth while servants hurried and scurried to various rooms carrying boots and coats.

He had not left her side since she had taken her seat next to him in the carriage. While his actions made her feel welcome and, dare she think it? Cared for? The same actions also made her feel her folly more acutely.

"Yes, we do," she agreed. That had been her whole purpose in walking to Netherfield today.

"Bingley," Mr. Darcy called.

Mr. Bingley was at his friend's side in an

instant. Was it always thus? Did Mr. Darcy call and expect his friends to immediately respond? She grimaced and pushed her questions aside. Had she learned nothing in the past fourteen hours? He had injured her pride at the assembly, and her pride needed to let go of its resentment. Mr. Darcy had apologized for his poor behaviour and had from that point forward acted as nothing but a perfect gentleman. She was the one at fault now, not him.

"May we use your study?" he was asking Mr. Bingley when Elizabeth finally stopped scolding herself long enough to pay attention to what was happening.

Mr. Bingley grinned from ear to ear, obviously pleased as punch to grant them the use of whichever room they wished to use. When he had finished saying as much to Mr. Darcy, he turned to Elizabeth.

"Are you chilled? Do you need dry stockings? My grandfather did not change his stockings after he returned from a damp morning of hunting and did not live more than a fortnight hence."

Elizabeth nearly giggled at the severely serious look on Mr. Bingley's face for it seemed so out of place with his character. "My stockings are dry, and I am no colder than I would be on any damp day in late October.

"I will send something warm to drink to the study for you."

"That would be most kind, Mr. Bingley."

"Think nothing of it," he said. "It is the least I can do to see to the wellbeing of a friend."

With that said, his serious mien dissolved into a more familiar smile. "I intend to host a ball, and I should be sorry if you were not able to attend because I did not see to your health."

"You are planning a ball?"

Bingley touched a finger to his lips. "My sister has not yet heard she is planning a ball." He winked and chuckled as he moved on to check on Charlotte and Mary.

Mr. Darcy held his hand out to her. "Miss Bingley will be thrilled to display her hosting ability to the neighbourhood. However, I doubt she will be as excited about having the neighbourhood dancing in her brother's house." He lowered his voice. "She thinks too highly of herself. Something which was one of my faults as well until it was pointed out to me just how rude it was." He squeezed her hand.

"I doubt you were ever excessively haughty," Elizabeth retorted.

Mr. Darcy shook his head. "I was arrogant enough to declare myself above giving consequence to young ladies who did not have dance partners without pausing to consider that the lack of a dance partner was no fault of the lady, but it was rather the fault of gentlemen, such as myself, who were not doing their duty."

"Does that mean, Mr. Darcy, that you will be dancing every set at Mr. Bingley's ball?" she teased.

Mr. Darcy chuckled. "If it will prove my worth to you, I will dance every set save two with a different lady all evening, and I will do so happily." He led her into Mr. Bingley's study and closed the door.

"All save two?" she asked as she surveyed the room. It was both tidier than her father's and tidier than she had expected from someone who was so agreeable as Mr. Bingley was. The room, however, was just as relaxed and friendly in appearance as the gentleman who now called this study his.

"Those two would be saved for you."

Elizabeth slowly turned her eyes from studying the empty shelves of one entirely neglected bookcase to Mr. Darcy.

"If you would have me."

She saw his chest lift and lower as his eyes searched hers. She shook her head in bewilderment.

"If *I* would have *you?* Sir, it is I who has behaved badly and should be asking you to forgive me and allow me to return to being one of your friends."

He took her by the arm and moved her toward the group of chairs in the far corner of the room.

"Your displeasure with me last evening is understandable."

"No, it is not," she declared. "You must allow me to wear the shame of my actions."

He motioned to a chair. "Please, be seated."

She did as he asked.

"Do not claim blame where it is not yours to claim," he said as he settled into the chair beside the one in which she sat.

He was an impossible man! She was attempting to be noble and bear her part of the wrong from last night's incident at Lucas Lodge. Why would he not let her?

"You did act without gathering all the facts. I will give you that."

She sighed in relief. "Thank you."

"However, your ability to gather those facts was hampered in no small way by my desire to conceal them."

"But you had a good reason!" she cried. That seemed to stop him from whatever else he was going to say, and the room lay silent for seven ticks of the clock that stood on the shelf behind them.

"How do you know that? I have not yet explained myself to you."

Oh! Elizabeth's stomach flipped. How did he not know that she knew about his sister and what Mr. Wickham had done?

"When he returned to Lucas Lodge last night,

did not Mr. Bingley tell you about visiting me?" She had been certain he was going to do so since he had mentioned hoping his friend would be forgiving.

Mr. Darcy shook his head. "I left Lucas Lodge after you did, and I would have departed for London that moment had my cousin not insisted I wait until the morning, which I will admit, given the lack of moonlight last night was a wise suggestion." He tipped his head. "When did Bingley visit you, and what did he tell you?"

"He did not tell you when he returned to Netherfield?"

Again, Mr. Darcy shook his head.

"And he did not mention it this morning?"

"Not a word."

How strange!

"I thought he would."

"He did not."

"Then, I suppose it is up to me to tell you."

"I suppose it is, unless you would like for me to call him."

"No! I can tell you." She glanced uneasily toward the door and drew the corner of her bottom lip between her teeth. "I hope he is not offended that I told you he visited me."

"Bingley?" Mr. Darcy's eyes were wide. "He has no right to be offended. This is his doing."

"Do not be angry with him. He acted in service to you." She drew a breath and after expelling it slowly, she began to tell Mr. Darcy how Mr. Bingley could not allow her to think of his friend as anything less than a gentleman.

"He told you about the living and that Wickham played with Georgiana's heart?" Mr. Darcy looked as if he could not quite believe what he was hearing.

Elizabeth nodded.

"Did he tell you that Wickham had convinced Georgiana to elope with him and it was only my fortuitous early arrival in Ramsgate which forestalled it?"

Elizabeth rested her hand on her heart as tears filled her eyes.

"No," she whispered.

How dreadful that must have been! No wonder Mr. Bingley had said that if Wickham's scheme had succeeded it would have destroyed

Mr. Darcy. Even now, she could see the pain in his expression. Cautiously, she moved her hand from her heart to rest it on his arm.

"How fortunate you were to be able to save her."

"It was none of my doing. It was fate that saved her, not me. I was the one who put her in harm's way."

"I cannot allow you to claim blame where it is not yours to claim." She smiled softly at him when he lifted startled eyes to her.

"But Richard and I hired Georgiana's companion, and it was through that companion that Wickham gained access to my sister." His jaw clenched, and he looked away from her. The struggle to keep his emotions regulated was evident in his expression. He was hurting, but he was not thinking clearly.

"Did you know this companion was duplicitous or did you know that she knew Mr. Wickham? Did you ask her when you interviewed her if she knew him or if she was planning to help coerce your sister into an elopement?"

Mr. Darcy blinked. "How would I know to ask those things?"

"How indeed?" Elizabeth replied and then fell silent as she watched his handsome features while he processed that thought.

The guilt and sorrow this man had born on his own caused Elizabeth's heart to ache. She longed to be able to take some of it from him and bear it herself. How she would love to be allowed the privilege to sit with him like this and help him navigate life. And in that thought, she found the truth she had been searching for since Mr. Bingley had visited her last night.

"I would choose you."

His brow furrowed. "I do not understand."

"Last night, Simon asked me to choose between you and him." She paused and allowed that thought to settle on him as she continued to admire his confused expression. Then, with her heart beating loudly in her ears and her cheeks aflame with heat, she confessed her whole heart to him. "After Mr. Bingley left me last night, I began to search my heart and have come to the conclusion that I would choose you, and not just above Simon, but above all others."

Mr. Darcy sat motionless with his lips parted slightly and his eyes locked on hers.

"Can I get you some wine?" she asked when he continued to look at her mutely.

He shook his head as if clearing a fog. "Did you just say you would choose me?" A small smile tugged the corners of his lips upward.

She sighed in relief. "Yes."

"Why?" he took hold of her hands. "Why would you choose me?"

"Because you allowed me to choose you – no, no, that is not true. You did not *allow* me to choose you. You *compelled* me to choose you. While your noble and caring character recommended you to me, you – your heart, your goodness, your whatever it is about you – captured my heart and made me love you."

"You love me?" A beautiful smile suffused his features.

She returned his smile as she nodded. "I do. I do not know how or when I came to love you, and I admit that I have only just recognized it for what it is, but yes, I do love you."

"You love me," he repeated in a tone of wonder. His brow furrowed as if he was thinking about something, but his smile did not diminish. "May I speak to your father and ask to court you?"

A burst of joyful laughter escaped Elizabeth. "You may ask him whatever you wish for my answer to you will never change. I will always choose you."

He rose from his chair and offered her his hand to help her rise. Then, to her surprised delight, he pulled her into his embrace. "You would truly court me?"

"Yes. Most happily." She drew in the scent of him. It was a mixture of spice and the out of doors that wrapped around her and welcomed her home. Here was where she belonged. This man was her future.

"And you would even marry me?"

"Yes, I would marry you." Was it truly so impossible for him to imagine that she would want him? The thought made her feel wonderfully cherished.

He drew back to look at her. "And you will dance two sets with me at Bingley's ball?"

"Three if you would allow it," she replied with a teasing smile.

"I would by no means suspend any pleasure of yours, Elizabeth." His eyes fell on her lips. "May I kiss you?"

The something wonderful which had hung around the edges of her mind for the past several days invaded every part of her being, filling her with a heady joy she had never even imagined existed. Mr. Darcy wished to dance with her, court her, marry her, and kiss her, and she had no desire to stop him from doing any of those things. Therefore, she once again borrowed his words.

"I would by no means suspend any pleasure of yours, Mr. Darcy."

He chuckled. "Call me Fitzwilliam." He placed a hand on her cheek and allowed his thumb to caress her bottom lip. "Say it again," he said in a soft and deep tone.

Her tongue touched his thumb as she wet her lips and swallowed. "I..." Oh, it was difficult to speak when he was still caressing her lip and looking at her with such obvious longing.

"I..." she began again, only cringing slightly at how breathy her voice sounded.

"I would by no means suspend any pleasure of yours, Fitzwilliam."

His thumb stopped moving on her lip and his hand, which had been resting on her cheek, gently tipped her chin up while his mouth lowered to meet hers. Tenderly he kissed her. Then, he lifted his mouth from hers but only enough to break contact, for she could feel his breath on her lips when he spoke.

"I love you, Elizabeth. From the moment you refused me at the assembly, I was lost to you, and I will happily remain so until the day I die." Then, he kissed her again, though more urgently.

"I do not think you will be needing this tea to warm you," Mr. Bingley said, breaking through the delicious haze that surrounded Elizabeth as Fitzwilliam kissed her.

Elizabeth buried her face in Darcy's chest.

"Oh, do not stop on my account," Mr. Bingley said with a chuckle, and Elizabeth dared to peek at him. He was grinning like a cat who had just caught a mouse.

"Get out," Mr. Darcy growled.

"Shall I tell the colonel that you will not be returning to town today?"

"Yes. Now, get out."

Mr. Bingley laughed. "I knew you two would be a good match. Did I not say so, Dearest?"

It was then, that Elizabeth noticed Jane standing at the door to the study.

"Indeed, you did, Mr. Bingley. And did I not tell you that you were right?"

"I believe you did." He held his arm out to Jane who placed her hand lightly on it. "Now, about the colonel," he said to Jane before winking at Darcy and Elizabeth as he closed the door.

Elizabeth looked at the gentleman she loved, who still held her. "Did he...?" She motioned between herself and her Fitzwilliam.

"He seems to think he did." He released her

and walked to the desk to get the tea Bingley had left there.

"What is it?" Elizabeth said, coming to stand next to him when he passed over the tea for a slip of paper that lay on the desk. She peered over his arm and read the missive.

Mr. Bingley,

I am giving this note to Ephraim just as we are leaving Longbourn. Lizzy is not a slow walker, so by the time you receive this, we will be nearing the old turning lane. If the colonel and his cousin leave upon your receiving this letter, they should greet us before it is too late to turn the coach around before Longbourn.

As you had suspected by Elizabeth's state of unrest last night, she is indeed in love with your friend, though she is too stubborn by half to admit it! However, we can hope that her good sense will bring you the success you seek in matching Mr. Darcy.

J.B.

"They matched us? Jane and Mr. Bingley matched us?" Elizabeth could barely believe what she had just read, but there it was in Jane's pretty hand on a lined piece of paper with neatly trimmed edges – just the sort of page on which Jane preferred to write.

"It seems they did." Fitzwilliam wrapped an arm around her and pulled her close to his side. "We shall have to thank them properly at some point."

"I suppose we will," Elizabeth agreed. She turned to face him, and he turned toward her. "Shall we have tea?"

He shook his head. "Not just yet." And with that, he once again drew her to him and kissed her.

Before You Go

If you enjoyed this book, be sure to let others know by leaving a review.

~*~*~

Want to know when another Sweet Possibilities story will be available?
You can always know what's new with my books by subscribing to my mailing list.
(There will, of course, be a thank you gift for joining because I think my readers are awesome!)
Book News from Leenie Brown
(bit.ly/LeenieBBookNews)

~*~*~

Turn the page to read an excerpt of another one of Leenie's books

Discovering Mr. Darcy
Excerpt

[Do you enjoy stories about meddling friends and relations who would do just about anything to see Darcy and Elizabeth matched? *Discovering Mr. Darcy* is just such a story.]

Chapter 1

"Fitzwilliam," Lady Catherine called to her nephew, Colonel Richard Fitzwilliam, as he passed the door to her sitting room. "Your call can wait," she said in answer to the reply she knew was coming.

Richard sighed and turned into the room.

"Just Fitzwilliam." Lady Catherine's tone was stern as she looked down her nose and made a brushing motion with her hand, indicating that her other nephew, Fitzwilliam Darcy, should leave the room. "Close the door," she called after him. She waited until it was latched and she heard footsteps moving away from the room. Then, she took Richard by the arm and pulled him further into the room.

"Sit." She motioned to a golden tufted chair on the edge of a grouping in front of a window that looked out onto the front garden of the house.

Richard rolled his eyes and did as instructed. It was pointless to do otherwise. Lady Catherine always had her way, or there was a price to pay. It was far cheaper and easier to just listen. "To what might I ascribe the honor of this private conference?" It was likely some matter regarding the groves that she wished him to see to during his stay, for a stay at Rosings was rarely one of pure leisure.

Lady Catherine's eyes narrowed at his cheeky tone, but she did not reprimand him for it. He was always attempting to stir her ire, but today, she would allow no such distractions. She stood near the window and tilted her head to peer out and around toward the door where Darcy was just exiting. "It is time he marries," she said.

"Darcy?" Richard's eyes grew wide in surprise. This was not the conversation he had expected. In fact, it was a conversation he had always wished to avoid — at least with his aunt, that is.

She nodded, and leaving her vantage point at the window, she took a seat across from her nephew. "Yes, Darcy. Georgiana is not getting any younger and will need someone besides just her brother to guide her through her first season."

"But Anne –" Richard began. He knew neither Darcy nor his cousin Anne wished to marry the other, and he was prepared to argue their points.

"Not Anne," Lady Catherine interrupted. "They would not suit."

"Pardon?" Richard was at a loss for words. His aunt had always insisted that Darcy would marry Anne. In fact, it was a supposed engagement that had kept Darcy from feeling a need to begin looking in earnest for a lady to help him secure his estate for future generations.

Lady Catherine picked at a small flower on

the arm of her chair as she avoided meeting his eyes. The supposed engagement to her daughter had been merely an elaborate ruse to prevent a most disastrous outcome for Darcy. "He was not ready to begin a family. I had to keep him from rushing forward into doing his duty somehow."

Richard's mouth dropped open and then snapped shut. There were still no coherent thoughts forming in his mind. What his aunt was currently saying was clashing with what she had always said previously. Had she not taunted Darcy about doing his duty by marrying Anne?

She shook her head as if reading his thoughts. "Darcy was never going to marry Anne, and Anne knew it."

Richard's brows furrowed, and his lips pursed into a perplexed scowl. "You will need to explain."

Lady Catherine rose and walked to the window. Darcy was still pacing in the front garden. She watched him take six long strides away and then back. One foot fell in front of the other in perfect time and in equal measure. It was very much who he was — proper, dignified, well-ordered. "I promised his mother that I would see him marry well and for love." She raised a brow at Richard, causing his mouth to snap shut on whatever exclamation of surprise he was about to utter. "When Darcy's father died, Darcy was not ready to take on the responsibilities of an estate and make a proper decision about a wife. He would have rushed pell-mell into an untenable marriage that would have perhaps resulted in a family, but not a happy one. He would have sat down, drawn up some supposed list of qualifications of a proper wife, and gone about the business as if he were hiring a maid — without one thought about the misery he would face as a result of his calculated methods." She tipped her head and gave Richard a firm look. "Do not tell me he would not have done so. You know as well as I that he puts duty before everything." She shook her head. "I still think he has no idea what sort of wife he requires."

Richard laughed. This conversation was not at all what he had dreaded it would be. In fact, it was proving to be rather entertaining. "And you do know what sort of wife he requires?"

Lady Catherine returned to her chair. "I do, and I have found her." She chuckled at the way Richard's mouth dropped open again. "What Darcy needs is a simple country miss with a keen mind."

"And you found her?" Richard asked incredulously. His aunt did not travel, and so far as he knew, there were no acceptable country misses who frequented Rosings.

Lady Catherine raised one shoulder and let it drop slightly. "I believe I have." She leaned forward as she prepared to tell him how she had done it. "My parson is the heir to an estate that is entailed — a distant cousin or some such thing. It is difficult at times to follow his meandering."

Richard raised a brow and smirked, earning a rap on the knee.

"I am not meandering."

Richard inclined his head in acceptance although the smirk did not fade from his lips.

"Anyway, this cousin has five daughters —

three of a good marriageable age and two just reaching it." She smiled as the smirk dropped from Richard's face and was replaced with amazement. Five was a substantial number of daughters. It was not the largest she had heard of but substantial none the less. "I sent Mr. Collins to find a wife from among them because I reasoned that if he should marry one, then the others might be asked to visit on occasion, and I might be able to select one for Darcy."

Richard shook his head. "How did you know these ladies would be simple country misses with intelligence?"

Lady Catherine shrugged and shook her head. "There was no guarantee that they would be, but Collins had said their father eschewed town and spent the chief portion of his time in his study. I thought it likely that at least one daughter might have inherited her father's love of books and learning."

Richard nodded. That made sense. It was unlikely that all five daughters would be completely unlike their father. "Was Collins successful?"

Lady Catherine laughed. "No, he was not, and I really should have known he would go about it wrong. He tends to bungle things; however, in his bungling, he has made my task of selection most easy." She laughed again. "She refused him — soundly, and she is not taken with Darcy. Quite the contrary. She thinks him proud." Her eyes fairly danced with mirth. "Collins did secure a wife, however, and Mrs. Collins happens to be the future Mrs. Darcy's particular friend. That is how I know so much about my choice. Mrs. Collins is a lovely lady, very sensible — quite the opposite of her husband."

Richard's head tilted to the side as things began to come together into a coherent plan. "Your parson has a guest."

A smile split Lady Catherine's face. "Upon my urging, he does."

"And she is the lady you have selected?"

Lady Catherine's brows flicked upward quickly. "Clever, is it not?"

"Diabolical," Richard replied dryly.

Lady Catherine shook her head. "Did you see

how quickly Darcy agreed to visit the parsonage? I assure you it is not because he has a fondness for my parson." She leaned forward again and spoke in a whisper. "He danced with her."

Richard blinked. "Darcy danced?" That did hold some weight then. Darcy did not dance with anyone outside of his close sphere of friends.

Lady Catherine gave a satisfied nod. "Danced and argued with her and then fled the area. He is smitten; mark my words." She rose and motioned for Richard to follow her. "Note how he acts on your call, and when they come for dinner this evening, flirt with her. You will see I am right."

Richard rested his hand on the door knob. "And if you are right, what then? If they have argued, it follows that one or both might not be willing to enter into a marriage."

"One does not have to be willing to enter a marriage for a marriage to happen," replied Lady Catherine with a sly grin.

"A compromise?" Richard could not help the

small bit of excitement he felt about the possibility of a sneak attack.

"I shall not admit to it now or later," said Lady Catherine. "But they will marry. We shall see to it."

Richard chuckled as he left the room. While Darcy might have managed to outmaneuver the ladies and their mama's in the ton, he would stand no chance against their aunt.

"You are smiling," Darcy noted as Richard joined him in the front garden. Smiling after the completion of an interview with Lady Catherine was not a typical response. Rubbing your temples and seeking fresh air like a drowning man was a more likely response. Though Lady Catherine could be quite pleasant and even indulgent at times, she was more often than not demanding when she required an interview.

"It is a pleasant day, and I have escaped from our aunt with no more than a lecture on doing my duty while in residence." It was not entirely truthful, but there was enough truth in the statement for Richard to speak without so much as a pang of conscience. In fact, there was something rather like anticipation stirring in him as he considered how he and his aunt might capture their quarry. He would do as instructed and make his observations, and then, armed with the proper intelligence, he and Lady Catherine would contrive a plan.

"Yes, well, your duty only involves touring the grounds." Darcy knew his duty, as his aunt saw it, was to become the owner of the grounds through marrying her daughter, Anne. It was a duty that he in no way wished to fulfill. He sighed and rubbed his temple, thankful that he was out in the fresh air.

Richard glanced at his cousin. "You should tell her of your refusal to marry Anne."

Darcy drew in a deep breath and expelled it. "I intend to do so before we leave, but to do it now would make our stay more than a little unpleasant."

Richard's brows furrowed. "You truly mean to tell her?" He had told Darcy to speak to his aunt on each occasion when they journeyed to Rosings. Darcy had always claimed he would when the time was right. However, the correct time never seemed to present itself.

Darcy nodded. "It is time I consider marrying in earnest. I am nearly thirty, and Pemberley needs an heir. It is best to think of that while there is still hope of securing a wife happily." There was an heir to produce for Pemberley, this was true, but it was not his real reason for considering marriage. No, that reason, the lady he wished to find a way to marry, was currently installed at the parsonage in Hunsford. He had tried to escape it. He had hidden away and surrounded himself with work. He had attended functions and the theater. He had done everything he could think of to avoid what his heart was telling him because his heart's wishes did not match with the list of wifely qualifications in his head.

Richard chuckled. "You think that with an estate the size of Pemberley and the looks of your father, you would have to force a lady into marrying you even if you were twice your age?" He shook his head. "I cannot think of any lady of my acquaintance who would refuse you."

"I am not eloquent," Darcy replied. "Ladies find my reserve off-putting."

"That is not without remedy. You have no trouble smiling and talking with Bingley or me."

"Both you and Charles are like brothers. I have no trouble speaking to Georgiana, either."

Richard twirled his walking stick in the air and slashed at a bush along the path. "I have seen you speak to ladies at soirees."

"I have been terse and often stumble over my thoughts." Darcy caught a loose stone with his toe and sent it skittering across the path. "I wish it were not so, but it is."

"The right woman will loosen your tongue." Richard gave him a sidelong appraising look. There was a slump to Darcy's shoulders as if he had already given up hope of ever being able to speak to the right lady. "Have you found a lady?"

Darcy blinked. "N-no," he stammered, his ears heating with embarrassment. He was certain from the twitch of his cousin's lips that his reply was not accepted. Hopefully, Richard would just let it pass. "Bingley thought he had found a lady." Perhaps turning the conversation to the plight of a friend would keep Richard from pursuing whether Darcy had found a lady.

Richard laughed. "Bingley always thinks he has found a lady. He is far too amiable." He took another swing at a bush. "But go on and tell me about her. What is she like?"

"Beautiful. Well-mannered. Amiable. However, she seemed indifferent, and so it was suggested that he forget her."

Richard stopped walking. A thought of a disturbing nature began to form in his mind as he recalled a discussion they had had on the way to Rosings. "This is the match you helped him avoid?"

Darcy nodded.

"So it was not her connections to which you objected?"

"No. I did not wish to see him in a marriage of unequal affections."

"And this lady was one he met in Hertfordshire?"

Darcy nodded. "Had she demonstrated even a small amount of preference, I would not have suggested a separation." He sighed. "I thought he would forget her. He has not."

Richard could not help noting the way Darcy spoke as if it were not just his friend who was affected. "Is there a way to discover if this lady was indeed indifferent or if a renewal of addresses might be welcomed?"

Darcy turned toward the parsonage that was just within view. "We could ask her sister."

"Miss Bennet?" asked Richard in surprise. Oh, this was becoming a complicated tangle to be unravelled if the Miss Bennet at the parsonage was the lady Darcy was considering marrying and if this Miss Bennet's sister had been injured by Bingley's removal from Netherfield. He shook his head as he realized that there might be one lady in all of England and its empire who would refuse a man like Darcy.

Acknowledgements

There are many who have had a part in the creation of this story. Some have read and commented on it. Some have proofread for grammatical errors and plot holes. Others have not even read the story and a few, I know, will never read it. However, their encouragement and belief in my ability, as well as their patience when I became cranky or when supper was late or the groceries ran low, was invaluable.

And so, I would like to say *thank you* to Zoe, Rose, Kristine, Ben, and Kyle, as well as Patrons at Patreon, who followed this story as it developed and waited, as patiently as one might do, from one Friday to the next to read a new chapter. I feel blessed through your help, support, and understanding.

I have not listed my dear husband in the above group because, to me, he deserves his own special thank you, for, without his somewhat pushy insistence that I start sharing my writing, none of my writing goals and dreams would have been met.

Other Leenie B Books

You can find all of Leenie's books at this link
bit.ly/LeenieBBooks
where you can explore the collections below
~*~
Other Pens, Mansfield Park
~*~
Touches of Austen Collection
~*~
Nature's Fury and Delights, Sweet Regency
Romance Novelette Anthologies
~*~
Sweet Possibilities
~*~
Dash of Darcy and Companions Collection
~*~
Marrying Elizabeth Series
~*~
Willow Hall Romances

~*~

The Choices Series

~*~

Darcy Family Holidays

~*~

Darcy and... An Austen-Inspired Collection

About the Author

Leenie Brown has always been a girl with an active imagination, which, while growing up, was both an asset, providing many hours of fun as she played out stories, and a liability, when her older sister and aunt would tell her frightening tales. At one time, they had her convinced Dracula lived in the trunk at the end of the bed she slept in when visiting her grandparents!

Although it has been years since she cowered in her bed in her grandparents' basement, she still has an imagination which occasionally runs away with her, and she feeds it now as she did then — by reading!

Her heroes, when growing up, were authors, and the worlds they painted with words were (and still are) her favourite playgrounds! Now, as an adult, she spends much of her time in the Regency world, playing with the characters from her favourite Jane Austen novels and those of her own creation.

When she is not traipsing down a trail in an attempt to keep up with her imagination, Leenie resides in the beautiful province of Nova Scotia with her two sons and her very own Mr. Brown (a wonderful mix of all the best of Darcy, Bingley, and Edmund with a healthy dose of the teasing Mr. Tilney and just a dash of the scolding Mr. Knightley).

Connect with Leenie

E-mail:
LeenieBrownAuthor@gmail.com
Facebook:
www.facebook.com/LeenieBrownAuthor
Blog:
leeniebrown.com
Patreon:
https://www.patreon.com/LeenieBrown
Subscribe to Leenie's Mailing List:
Book News from Leenie Brown
(bit.ly/LeenieBBookNews)

www.ingramcontent.com/pod-product-compliance
Lightning Source LLC
Chambersburg PA
CBHW060415180626
46817CB00007B/2586